"One of the most innovative and enchanting books of recent time. . . . [Gordon] has constructed a novel in dictionary form in which ordinary words reveal secret worlds that cling passionately to one another in a merry, whirling, lexical dance."
—Thomas Christensen, *San Francisco Chronicle*

"Karen Gordon has composed a pseudo-dictionary of allusive definitions or definitive allusions, strongly evoking Raymond Queneau. When you think of the indignant squeals from Pollyanna reviewers if anyone does anything in the merest way original, Ms. Gordon deserves a hurrah and a bow; she is witty, climactic, and invasive, and she can even make you homesick for Paris."
—Paul West

"I was immensely impressed with *The Red Shoes*, so ingenious, as if Ambrose Bierce wrote *Pale Fire*! It is far too witty and illuminatingly scholarly—while a brilliant novel—to be mistaken for the dryasdust library-work of a Yale professor, for it is alive and alert."
—Alexander Theroux

"The most admirable thing that I can imagine is to make a book unlike any book ever written, but a book that will immediately seem a classic. That's what Gordon has done. I was showing a friend the book, and he asked me who's this Karen Gordon, etc., and I told him—it just popped out of my head—'she's a kind of Lady Rabelais.' What I had in mind is that combination of intelligence, irreverence, learning, wit, bawdiness, humor, and outrageous story-telling."
—Charles Simic

"Sensual and surreal, *The Red Shoes* proposes fictional marzipans, prose for lovers in the form of *friandises*. To be relished *comme une coupe de plaisir*."
—Rikki Ducornet

"A fabulous fabrication, stitched word by word into a garment made of ecstatic flannel, wrinkled linen moods and garnished with a sexy silk narrative handkerchief. It's a lexiphile's dream."
—Pat Nolan, *Poetry Flash*

"Gordon ransacks fairy tales, movies and popular romances to show how words' associations filter into the culture; in so doing, she holds a mirror to the stock language of everyday conversations and the non sequiturs and reflexive clichés that mar much prose."
—*Publishers Weekly*

Karen Elizabeth Gordon

THE RED SHOES
and other tattered tales

Dalkey Archive Press

First published, in radically different form, as *Intimate Apparel: A Dictionary of the Senses* (Times Books, 1989). Several of Yolanta's postcards first appeared in *Exquisite Corpse* in 1983. Gretl, Red Shoes, and the little match girl came out in *Fiction Network* in 1988 before finding themselves in *Intimate Apparel*.

Library of Congress Cataloging-in-Publication Data

Gordon, Karen Elizabeth.
    [Intimate apparel]
    The red shoes and other tattered tales / Karen Elizabeth Gordon.
        p. cm.
    First published as: Intimate apparel. 1989.
    I. Title.
PS3557.O66837I58   1996   813'.54—dc20   95-25958
ISBN 1-56478-092-9

Partially funded by grants from the National Endowment for the Arts and the Illinois Arts Council.

Dalkey Archive Press
Illinois State University
Campus Box 4241
Normal, IL 61790-4241

NATIONAL
ENDOWMENT
FOR ❤ THE
ARTS

INTRODUCTION

Ah, nothing in this world we live and dream is only what it seems. Here you have a dictionary that is *really* a storybook without a proper ending—just a provocative, improper one. The stories in this rattled box do not so much break off as become attached to one another, while you become attached to them, and to the characters whose stories they are: the hapless hypochondriac with his faulty kneecap and bar of anodyne soap; Bedruthan with *his* knees knocking in fear at the ocean's frothy edge, and the deadpan, deadly sensuous mermaid he seeks, to return a lost tortoiseshell comb; Yolanta expatriating on the Continent with her *langue maternelle*, her passport—and a bookmark between her legs; a sassy Cinderella, lost in reveries, breaking glasses in the dishwater, and unmasking social form and ceremony in her unabashed dealings with the prince; and many, many others, weaving in and out of each other while the two seamstresses, Elsbeth of the North and Anja of the South, stitch together their tattered tales and scattered lives into a fabrication they can *all* wear at once upon a time. And so can you. Baffled, perhaps, at first, you will find that you are slipping, slowly but silkily, into something more comfortable the further you read, the more familiar you become. Because this is an affectionate book that wants to be held, like any woman within it, and will hold your attention and call it back again to fulfill this most agreeable desire.

Fabric, fabrication—such is the stuff of these lost chronicles come together here. Swinging their hatboxes, swaying their hips, chapters with torn slips wander in on high heels and blistered feet. A wedding dress is being cut out and sewn by the same two seamstresses who are handstitching all these pieces into place, with time and meaning layered like the ultimate wedding cake.* A cloth of many colors unravels, interwoven as it is of the simply real, the fabulously real, and the purely imaginary, and the threads, of various lengths and gleamings—well, some are invisible, so a nearsighted *coutu-rière* bent over them has declared. A cloth of ecstatic flannel, narrative handkerchief, and wrinkled linen moods; fur hands, satin of solitude, handled-with-carelessness glass shoes. Out of a tailor's dummy's muslin epidermis is the flesh made word.

Words themselves are the intimate attire of thoughts and feelings. Here they are turned inside-out to see what's going on beneath the surface of everyday presences, garments and forms. And if a book can wear a jacket, the notion of a book can be turned inside-out, too—for much of the *story* here is in the notes, and not in the body of the text . . . the very body we find on the final undulation: nude with sunbeam for zipper. Facing things in this manner, we watch estrangements disappear. Death, whose name we avoid pronouncing, is just the girl next door.

Like a diaphanous nightgown, language both hides and reveals. There is no way of getting at the naked truth, even if it's wearing the Emperor's New Clothes, or the Empress's New Clothos. We follow our Mother Tongue into her bou-doir, anyway, hoping for a glimpse of something never yet beheld—and come face to face with our own reflections in her most private mirror, veiled meanings in a gossamer heap on the floor. And still there are enough words left in the old girl's voice to sing us to sleep once again. "I've got *you* un-covered," she says.

*There are lots of cakes, being created and consumed, and cookie crumbs on the sheets of the alphabed. In *The Gingerbread Varia-tions*, the cake itself is a consumer of lost little souls, the sweet tooth of childhood zigzagging them through the woods.

DRAMATIS PERSONAE

Anja, a wanderlusting seamstress from Croatia, whose territorial seams are in confusion of late. It is thanks to Anja's chance find (a tailor's dummy stuffed with shredded manuscripts) that these tales have come to light and are taking some sort of shape—as she sorts and stitches their tatters with her Scandinavian colleague, Elsbeth.

Bedruthan, a reluctant romantic—and gigantic—hero of Cornish coast and legend, courageously searching for a mermaid whose only property has floated into his hands (or did he find it in the sands?).

Cinderella, resiliently abused stepchild whose secret rebellions in both fact and fantasy forge her liberty. Seeing past mere wish fulfillment, she unmasks social form and ceremony in her unabashed dealings with the prince.

Columbine, a commedia dell' arte trouper in contempo clothing who performs with her rowdy pals Pantalone, Pedrolino, Grattiano, Arlecchino, Burattino, Flavinia, and Franceschina on both sides of the Adriatic.

Effie (short for Ephemera, and the twin sister of Errata), a Mediterranean nymph pursued by a faun who looks like Blaise Cendrars.

Elsbeth, Anja's Danish collaborator, whose niece is enjoying a strange captivity: the red shoes, running us all amok. Elsbeth once floored a quipspeak critic for saying this book is coming apart at the seamstresses. It's coming together, she solemnly avers.

Hansel and **Gretl**, siblings with the usual spats until they unite in their plot to overthrow *The Gingerbread Variations* witch. For once, however, we see that sorceress's side of the story, too: at least one grim glimpse.

Jacob Other, linguist, pan-discipline critic, poet, novelist, occasional usher at the Opéra. Fast friends with fellow expatriate Yolanta, whom he met in a *boulangerie*.

Jonquil Mapp, oscillating inamorata of Torquil. Got her B.A. in geography from Amplochacha U.

Little match girl, locked out of the Nordic holidays, selling matches and burning her frozen fingers, hallucinating from cold and hunger, telling her Dark Night of the Body to us all.

Morpheus, god of dreams, invoked, supplicated, wooed by our insomniac author.

Red Shoes didn't stand still long enough for us to get a good description.

Timofey, precociously fed on Slavic lit, later the lover of Nadia—but now he's a specter afraid of the dark, at work on his own posthumous lexicon.

Torquil, Jonquil's weekend roustabout after their first carnal marathon at the Last Judgment Pinball Machine Motel.

Yolanta, raving bibliophile, expatriate writer and Paris correspondent for *Exquisite Corpse*. Does translations when desperate, strikes many as ill-mannered (the French as *mal élevée*), although the baker defends her character and keeps a shelf of books behind his *baguettes* so as not to disrupt her delusions.

SUPPORTING (and cavorting) CAST includes:

A penguin who sniffs perfume, a clochard who steals gloves, a femme fatale who steals bouquets. An innkeeping couple on the road through the Balkans, a doctor in Baden-Baden, a pig and a hermit named Henri. An apparition who brings his custom to Anja, as Hans Christian Andersen does to Elsbeth. A peasant and his wild young bride attracted to the ocean. (He's an aficionado of metafiction, she of swift sensations.) Another peasant with a shoe to repair and a balletomanic daughter. Many cows, most of them lowing, one dead (on a bus). A hypochondriac with jet-set appointments. An unidentified neuter pronoun with wet feet and a taste for beer. A blini woman who supports her *own* cast of characters on the road in Mother Russia. Don Juanita heats up the socks, but not in the laundromat with poker players or with the milliner, once a shivering model. A man in a red cape poses a mild threat and provides the musical background.

All knowledge has its origins in sensations.
                    —Saint Thomas Aquinas

If my knife had followed your foot's outline, could the fit of
this shoe have been nicer?
                    —Herondas

ABSINTHE

She drenched him with an absinthe
regard.

See **dusk; lips**.
　Well, you don't have to. I'll tell you right now that she proceeded to let out a wild shrill hiccup, and when we kept question-
ing her about the parchment enwrapping her salmon, and the lost
Albanian, she excused herself to the powder room "and galloped
off in a chorus of evasive whispers."
　But you'll find yourself in their company again soon enough,
wondering if dessert will *ever* arrive so he can lean across the table
to ask, "Don't you want the rest of your clafouti?" and rend its
remains with his fork.

ACT

It was a meaningless act, but
we knew its implications.

"a meaningless act"
   One of the propositions subjected to philosophic inquiry in
Carnal Knowledge. "The closeness that comes in handfuls" eludes
one's grasp when "the metaphysical stuff gets out of hand."

BABUSHKA

"Here, they just didn't get dry enough," he said with concern for her warfare as he dabbed at her tears with a corner of her own babushka, which could also turn into a flour sack* should the shortage of occasion demand.

*Usually it was a fine buckwheat flour, for blini were popular in her movable household of men, women, and children dangling from her apron, and pots and pans clanging against their helmets and bulletproof vests.**

Not versts, which they traveled many of sometimes of a day; of others, they might not stray far from the sizzling butter, the sour cream, and the caviar* beside a river flowing off the page. .   .   .   .

The caviar, it must be noted, was a matter of robbery, for the routes they followed were those of the Beluga merchants and not of Chichikov.*

****Just picture this one as the flapping of an inside-out overcoat whose lining, empty of any particular soul, could propel his droshky around a Mother Russia no one had ever swerved through, breaking off whole chapters of a novel-in-progress as countless talented and invisible serfs fell into the . .   .   .

They camped out in pockets of the Motherland's big apron. Don't see **pockets**.

BEAST

Down the alley slouched a beast
en route to the Apocalypse.

Not all that rough a beast, this one. He had shaved that morning,
and his swagging carriage made alluring ripples in the silk T-shirt
on his back.

BELT

(from *The Red Shoes*)

What could she do but lavish attention on them, accursed though they might be? She bought a red leather purse and belt to match them, a pleated hound's-tooth skirt. She polished and buffed them, smoothed over each scuff as well as she could; and when they needed resoling or were down at the heels, she wore them to the cobbler's and spent the night there if he couldn't get to them right away. Every year she sent the cobbler a greeting card on Saint Crispin's Day, a gesture that never occurred to his other customers, and she wore galoshes when it rained.

In Ingmar Bergman's film* of *The Red Shoes*, they (Liv, Erland, Bibi, even Sven) are wearing scratchy scarves and distressing shoes, and are expressing lots of angst. After the movie, a kiosk opens in the lobby so that members of the audience can buy their very own red shoes and then have something to point to accusingly in their woes and sufferings. See **pain**.

*Bergman's films also figure in the virgin-spring-and-allish sequel to the patisserisqué foreplay of **jar**:

> He stretched out her shortcake, he tamed her wild strawberries, he was her smiles of a summer knight in blinding ardor.

BODICE

As the pale author banged out pastoral prose in her darkened chamber on the conjugal bed, her impostor scampered among the nasturtiums, crunching the delightful papery flames of their petals and the peppery leaves, rolling in them, running them through her fingers, and stuffing them into her bodice thumping with abundance and greed.

BOOKS

The beautiful bones of Notre Dame crouch and soar in the light flooding stone and I shove myself through the door of Shakespeare and Company to read about Madame de Pompadour's love potions and the many-colored solitudes of Emily Dickinson. A swarthy English-speaking type approaches me, in unctuous wonder first at where we've met before, then why I could possibly like to read, arriving at his own inspired conclusion that "it must be something psychological," with which I can only agree. I ensconce myself in a chair but am soon to be lifted out of this attitude by an invitation to the library above. "I must lie down where all the ladders start, in the foul rag-and-bone shop of the heart" points the way up a rough red stairway which is to be crawled, not walked, into a dimly lit affable claustrophobia of old books, ghosts, and somnambulists, big chairs in corners of sunken, slumbering structure, and a bed against one wall, covered in blue velvet and summoning up all the bibliophiles who must have sated their lusts in this room. I lean back and gratify some of my own, in a rapid succession of imaginary lovers who dematerialize after having their way with me and stealing a few books.

From Yolanta's PARIS column for *Exquisite Corpse*, that first "crossed legs in closed winter" year of exile and uncertainty, adventure and thwarted love. Expatriate translator, writer, and drifter, and Jacob's* Neoplatonic other, Yolanta is the eventual author of these motley collected works:

> *The Scarlet Slippers*
> *The Read Letter*
> *Maps and Tatters*
> *A Crusty Baguette, a Cup of Beaujolais*
> *You Darling Manflower: A Bestiary*
> *Crossed Legs and Closet Winters*

*Jacob Other: a would-be Renaissance man, but for his lumbosacral strain. Three times resisted Yolanta's entreaties that he consult the physician in Baden-Baden so highly recommended by other afflicted characters in this book.

BOOTS

AT WAR WITH ONESELF OR OTHERS,
IT'S ALL THE SAME TO ME

The foxholes were all full, and I was naked, alone, and alarmed. Shots swam past me in slow motion. I was the missing mark. Beneath my footfalls lay the best of bargains: terra firma, half dead or asleep. My boots were muddy, my face was a mess, but I was too cold to care, and why should I look any better in a rifle's line of sight? I was glad I'd chosen the First World War to be in because it was easier then to get around on foot, and I could speak a little French. In the trench. I looked around for my buddies but they were neither dead nor alive and so I sat around waiting for my brother who was born after the Second World War, two years ahead of me, because I was fighting before my time had come.

"my boots were muddy"
   During another, less metaphorical visit in France (the reverie is from her bestiary), Yolanta ate her way through the back streets of Paris ("off the eaten path") for the book *A Crusty Baguette, a Cup of Beaujolais*:

> Last night I walked down rue de Bellechasse to La Sologne, a restaurant that chose the right street, for everything they serve once ran wild—little birds brought together into *confits*, small furred creatures I couldn't translate into English or back to life, grouse, *morilles*, berries, forest seeds. The place was rather like a lodge in the woods, and the welcome as if I were knocking the mud off my boots and hanging up my shotgun to tuck in for a bit of warmth in the dark winter's night. And so the bright berries and *cheminée*. Once before, while ogling the young deer in bitter chocolate at the adjoining table, and three tiny American children tending to their *plats* with interest, then to their mousses with lust, I dined on wild baby boar in a light, tangy sauce with bacon, mushrooms, over

fresh pasta in two colors and surrounded by a ruby ring of
fresh cranberries. Last night, though, no craving to sink my
teeth into savage flesh, so I had several hors d'oeuvres, deli-
cate, dusky mixtures of wild vegetables and herbs, and, well—
one bone to toss to the carnivore in me—a bed of spinach
and herbs with thin slices of white pheasant meat.

BOOTS

(from *The Little Match Girl*)

My Russian grandmother sat in the corner
with her red boots listening to the wolves.

"My Russian grandmother"
   Vasilisa, who, in her younger days, loved to bully her husband
Vanya by making him eat much more kasha than he wanted and by
taking up the choicest spot in their house on the steppes. He would
come home with his ax to find her flattened out on the stove
whose belly he had been out finding provisions for, as he would be
on the following day, too, and every day of the long winter that
came and went year after year. As the howling wolves announce
more eloquently than a bit of crepe sewn to the edge of the page,
this booted baba is one of the last grandmas in the little match
girl's hallucinations brought on by hunger and the approach of
death. Vasilisa, her red boots comfortably propped on a low table
groaning with zakuski,* comes hard on the heels of a tough old
Serb with paprikas strung over her shoulders and blisters on her
feet; grandmothers with fingers stained from turmeric, raspberries,
and Turkish cigarettes; grandmothers in yashmaks, sarongs, kimo-
nos, negligées; and a Betty Crocker grandmother, her apron dusted
with flour, grieving for the unfinished cookie, and up to her elbows
in chopped walnuts and chocolate chips.

*Oh, God, I wish I were eating
some right now!

BOUDOIR

He followed her into the delphiniums and irises of her private wallpaper and began speaking to her back and her three reflections, all wearing a pout—or a scowl—or was she biting her lip?

See the **mug** of reconciliation.

BRA

I say! How can I excite you to these raptures regarding the celestial machine, that mechanical angel duck, that brought me here from Boulogne, skim you along all the sensory impressions playing on me since my arrival ("She longed to go to England, to the land of Christopher Smart, to inhale the noxious vapours that nourished his exalted soul")? Looks in the streets of London are furtive, disarming after the outright unwrappings a woman undergoes in Paris—I used to walk out of a *métro* car fumbling at my buttons and the hook of my bra strap, so surely did they feel undone, so shimmeringly did I sometimes feel sated of a steamy afternoon (name of *métro* line: Erotic Transport)—but my eyes are agog here, anyway, watching, for one thing, streets changing their names in the middle of puddles (yesterday I went on a Plague Walk), and sounds, too, have struck me, like the footsteps, with clipped, working-class accents, leaving for home at five o'clock. At night, the rumble of trains in Waterloo Station rattles the window where I sleep, and I half expect to wake up one morning halfway to Scotland in a bed of damp heather beside a track of British Rail. Must get gussied up in a hurry and start queuing up in the West End. By God, I believe this *is* the time I imagine I'm having!

Love,
Yolanta

BREAD

A couple of *pains de campagne* (*pas trop cuits*)* on her feet,
and wrapped in a semblance of sanity she had donned for her
matutinal tour of the *quartier*, Yolanta entered the *boulangerie*
on the corner and requested a copy of *Manon Lescaut*.

*Peasant bread (not too crisp).

Jacob Other, visiting Yolanta one afternoon in her *chambre de
bonne*, found her popping two battered books into the toaster when
he arrived for tea. The incident turned up in his essay (brief, as
usual) "Déconfitures et tartines," which ended, perhaps because of
the marmalade on her nightstand, "It all remains to be seen
through; she is so good at guesswork she'll never put clothes on or
find a literal** meaning on the other side of the bed."
    It was someone else, anyway, eating a toasted page in **lips**.

**Yolanta had given some thought to the closeness in French of
lire (to read) and *délire* (delirium), and the presence of a bed (*lit*) in
literature.

BUBBLES

(from *The Glass Shoe*)

Dear Father,

How you ever came to lay your head among the bosoms of this family is beyond my wildest comprehension. I am trying, but my thoughts buckle back each time to the more essential question: how could you leave me here? I am writing to you at the end of my staggering day's work (yes, I sometimes stagger from exhaustion and hunger, for they feed me but poorly, and leave few crumbs on the white lacquer breakfast trays for me to scrape up on the way to the dishwater and the window that meets my gaze above the hot bubbles in the morning sun—such lovely rainbows on those swelling edges before they pop!). How often I have to remind myself that "This, too, shall pass," your words, and all that remains to fill the emptiness where once you were, with your dark and bracing odor and evening armchair repose like an animal after feeding at dusk.

After you left, they dropped all pretense of treating me as one of them, an accord I did not entirely rejoice in, anyway, as you will remember—you saw those sullen looks of accusation I would cast in your direction as I rolled little balls of bread along the edges of my plate and strained the dancing bubbles of mineral water through my teeth—and turned me into their fuliginous servant girl in overalls, with reddened knuckles and cracked heels. Before the others are stirring, I must be up and get the fire going, put out the milk bottles, and then I'm ladling the soured milk into bowls; baking brioche; grinding the coffee; tossing more wood onto the fire (wood I drag back from long rambles in the forest, in a cart that I pull like a frail young ox, swaying my head from side to side with my feet pointed outward to help keep my balance and keep from overturning the little logs already neatly stacked and crackling in the late summer sun); heating the day's first kettle of water over the merry flames for the coffee and all three sponge-baths I slather over each one as she lumbers out of sleep. I know that this ritual gives them the most satisfaction, allowing them to observe my humiliation up close—and then afterward there are the massages, as if I hadn't had enough with kneading the brioche and then the baguettes before tucking them under my own comforter to rise in the fresh memory of my own sleepy warmth.

I spend my days slaving over their bodies, jumping every time one of them yells, "Hey, Ashtray!" scrubbing the house and polishing the mirrors and silver, preparing these luscious snacks, and living for those moments to myself when I am off on an errand in the village or am left alone while the three of them are out paying a call. You know that my disposition has always been bright, no matter what adversity comes along to tarnish my twinkle, that I always find some small pleasure to cup in my hands. And so I gnaw at the bones of my misfortune and count my *blessures* in the evanescent gleams of copper, soap, and glass. Father, dear, I am very tired, and must close up for the night. In my dreams, your hand holds the meaning of all this suffering, which I know cannot outlast my beauty and my youth.

"*Hey, Ashtray!*"
    Some of their other nicknames for her were Dustrag, Mopsy, and Smudge. In one of her bubbly lamentations, Cinderella sighs, "I am a soap bottle in a flowered dress." So you see, she didn't *always* wear overalls. See **schmatte**.

"*And so I gnaw at the bones of my misfortune*"
    In *The Little Match Girl*, it's:

    "I was so hungry I started gnawing at my cuticles."

BUTTON

She buttoned up the house, folded it, stuffed it into her purse, locked the front door, and entered the foot traffic flowing past the secret dwelling no mugger would ever guess she now had clenched in her fist.

"folded it"
    See also **stars, wedding train,** and note to **slip.** And **kimono,** turning a body inside out.

In the carnival scene of *The Toes of Nichevo* we have:

> Hard on the heels of the pickpocket came a button collector through the crowd.

The part of the button collector was danced by Poco Rabinowitz, who in **macaroni** plays himself, a faun in camouflage rolling his eyes while the nymph, a friend of Effie's named Strophe, strips the surrounding foliage of vegetal parasites for the ongoing cosmetic experiments that so absorb the nymphs in their streams and glades.

CAKE

Eat your cake and make it too.

"Eat your cake"
   An entry in the diary as the big night approached suggests that
Cinderella intended to do so:

> "It's almost time to go to the ball, to get all glittered up
> (that'll pop their eyes out!) and hot under the arms, to sweat
> on the prince against his buttoned-up front while his hand
> slides down the back of my gown. Oh prince oh baby jump on
> me! Take me home to my *belle-mère* and my castle in the air,*
> and you'll sleep in my hair that even now unwinds to turn
> back time and polish the years in the suds the ashes and
> tears.** Your face on my belly, we'll calm down and discuss
> our wedding cake and how to frost it and how to cut our
> guests. How many little princes shall we beget and throw
> upon the land to slide down the banisters of our multilayered
> *gâteau de noce* with its moat of many colors running red with
> blood and blue, while I go barefoot, no more defective cloth-
> ing on my body, and sleep, oh yes, till noon."

*The author of *Reflections on a Slivered Shoe* must have been thinking of this passage when he wrote, "She stuck her foot in the firma-
ment."

**Another diary entry: "Had a good long sob today. Well, not so
much that I had to put out my little sign that says WET FLOOR."

CAKE

(from *The Gingerbread Variations*)

She had a handsome profile and lived in a *gâteau* of her own
making that she redecorated once a year, reinforcing the
sagging sidings of gingerbread, spackling fissures with a
vanilla glaze, and refrosting the entire façade with a design
she would work out in the fall and winter months after plant-
ing the bulbs.

CANDY

Don't get me started on Alfred again.
He showed up here the other night with
little paper bags over his ears.
How come? I says.
Want some penny candy, he says,
Your red-hot cinnamon heart.

"paper bags"
    In "The Introverted Attitude of the Intuitive-Feeling Type,"
a study of creativity by Jacob Other, we find: "He beats her and
kicks her and she smiles on, clutching messages in paper bags."
It's actually about someone enjoying a good night's sleep.

CAP

She knitted a loud woolen cap of her
recriminations and yanked it over his head.

She was already wearing a piece of silly headgear, I guess (well,
someone has to keep the milliner in grub and finery—see first **salt**),
because the scene continues:

> "You're not miffed, are you?" he asked, taking a cautious peep
> into her bonnet as a bank of nimbus clouds rolled forth from
> its brim.

CAPE

The man in the red cape put on Mozart's Divertimento in D Major (K. 136), rummaged around in his sewing basket for a spool of scarlet thread, made a double *Kaffee mit Schlag*, and, as Saint Martin gamboled about in the melodic fields, addressed himself to the fraying matter of his hood.

One of many quiet moments with himself when he's not out stalking and frightening little girls, or is it sturdy *Hausfrauen* he pursues? Tenderly domestic and very particular about the arrangement of his cottage, his recordings of Mozart and Schubert, the laundering of his shirts hanging all over the place to dry. Rather full around the hips. Just enough to affect his movements, the swish of his cape. Never short of invitations. See **pelisse**.

CIRCLE

They were running viscous circles around each other in the depths of the treacle well.

CLOUD

In the years, though, leading up to his demise—and you will remember that this was of his own free will, even if you don't agree that one has the right to take one's own life in the belief that that might make one feel better—the hypochondriac derived joy from small miracles, and never looked for the black clouds over the silver linings that would suddenly appear in his skies. One such fine day, his aberrant kneecap was not troubling him much, so he skipped to the loo.

"aberrant kneecap"
    For those readers who missed his pages in *The Transitive Vampire*—wearing shifting tenses, and a stoppered bottle—or those on whom the synopsis of his full tragedy left no lasting impression, it is repeated here:

> This story recounts the adventures of a hypochondriac who has been plagued by an aberrant kneecap and had tried several miracle cures and then takes matters into his own hands and drowned himself.

While we're at it: Timofey, the sempiternal lexicographer, appears in the early pages, and elsewhere in that same book, as the quaking hero of two other literary works.

COAT

A fine coat of lust lay over every thoughtful surface of the room.

This could be either Cinderella, out of her **drawers**, or Jonquil, thinking of love as "a little adventure looking for the right surface to happen upon" and "stretching myself out, in case someone wants to leave a message plastered to my body."

⤳ ⤴

"The Asinine Menagerie" is puzzling: a reworking of a La Fontaine (misspelled here, however, for some reason, as La Fontagne—I don't know about this girl's French, or was she dreaming of Chamonix?) fable, with the animals all transported to the Arctic North and wearing coats made of other animals' fur.

"The Asinine Menagerie"
  Another review by Jacob Other. Always short. "Form follows malfunction," Jacob says, pointing to his bad back and the curtness of his own critical style. His one essay on visual art produced the epigram "Art is only abstract when you look the other way."

COFFEE

The waitress frisked her between her coffee and her raised eyebrows.

See the first, the lonely **table**.

⤻ ⤻

Alexander Pope, who had a constant headache during the long disease his life, used to sniff coffee all day long and nights in public houses to relieve the pulsing pain. Like alcohol, coffee is a social drink: people are always asking, "Do you want a cup of coffee?" when they mean, "I wanna drag you to my bed." Coffee is also a necessary ritual between the sheets and streets. Bach wrote a piece called *The Coffee Cantata* whose raucous laughter and jollity we can only attribute to the magic of the drug. It's about a father who won't let his daughter marry unless she gives up drinking coffee, but she outsmarts the old man and has coffee written into the marriage articles, and becomes the first bride in history to live happily ever after.

Galloping ahead to Istanbul before *Frangipani's Pajamas*, this footnote is wondering if Bach was aware of the Ottoman marriage laws, and how graciously and seriously they granted a wife a lifetime of coffee in exchange for her total submission.

COLLAR

(from *The Red Shoes*)

The silhouette was jerking its head and munching its collar as its coach rolled past Daphne's darkened door.

Anja (see **frock**) didn't much care to take in work from apparitions, shadows, and other nebulous beings, but this one was so lightweight and mild-mannered, except for a fervent feeling about sound sartorial sensuousness, and a profound respect for her craft, and came the first time with his own sketch of the shirt he wanted, including some elaborate notions about the collar* to hide a birthmark at his throat, that Anja accepted the wad of dinars he pressed into her palm and agreed to the rest of his reasonable terms.

*The same collar, perhaps, that turns up in Elsbeth's painterly portrait of her still unseen, faceless friend:

> "Anja took a pin out of her mouth and jabbed it into a collar that lay in a curve in her lap. The rays of a setting sun caught on the edge of a silver box containing buttons and snaps and a lozenge for last winter's sore throat."**

See note to **scarf.

COMB

Bedruthan stepped lightly into the creamy waves clabbering
the black rocks of the Cornish coast. His huge body was un-
balanced by this even more enormous, oceanic motion and
by the disorienting configuration of cliffs fringed with gentle
green grass that twinkled in the early morning light like
Elfina's eyes, and gorse that prickled his calves and ankles
when he exposed them to the sweet climes of May. *This* was
a peculiar sensation, though: terrified of the water, never
before had he dared come this far into the foam crashing
around his knees, which knocked together while his teeth
met in desperate intervals. What mattered now, however,
even more than his old trepidation, was that he find the
mermaid whose comb* had washed up on the coarse sand.

*Had it paused in tidepools, to comb the fingers of sea anemones
and tease the gelatinous amethyst defenses beneath that enticing
act? Scraped the backs of starfish along spiny radii from point to
center to point? The comb, made of real tortoiseshell, just like the
tortoise Arthur Gordon Pym had eaten, was so tiny in his big rough
hands.**

**Bedruthan had problems with dry skin and chapping. When he
was a child, his father had smeared his hands with lamb fat (collected from the drippings caught in the preparation of the evening
meal) and then covered this mess with socks. (Funny, these, too,
came from sheep, the very ones who grazed a bit further inland, in
Devon, but since these giants' legs reached into the very skies
where the vigorous little depressions come from that are respon-
sible for the vicissitudes of the English weather, it took no time at
all to skip over there and return with a lamb or two kicking and
bleating beneath the provider's armpit.) And in these socks he
stuck Bedruthan's chafed paws as he tucked the little giant into his
bed.***

***Little Bedruthan slept in a bed modeled after the Viking ones
you can see to this day in the open-air museum outside Oslo and

while you're at it ponder the origins of the pillow, that handy prop on the connubial couch. The Vikings slept in beds that rose up at an angle, lifting the torso of one or another of these pillaging brutes**** higher than his lower half.

****Well, they weren't all brutes; most, in fact, were peaceful settlers seeking new breezes in which to set up house. But the brutes—did they, too, sometimes stray through the salted waters with lost baubles and bottles of eau de toilette looking for the nereids from whose nacreous grasp these objects had slipped? Did they ever feel anything like tenderness before the drenched beauty of these pelagic girlbeasts whose skin was kept atomized and luminous by spray just like the modern French mannequin's face fogged with Evian? And did these creatures grab their combs when they saw the prows bobbing up and down, and start sorting the algae and bracken out of their hair and rubbing the barnacles off the napes of their necks? Bedruthan wondered this and many other things to disport his attention far from his faltering steps.

"find the mermaid"
  Deep blue cheesecake. A girl with long hair waving about in the water and very scaly skin below the waist, despite hours spent in her grotty boudoir trying to make it sleek. Knocking about the Seven Seas and more, adrift in the Gulf Stream off England. In *Frangipani's Pajamas*, back to the Bosporus!

"nacreous"
  From the same mother as Pearl.

"fogged with Evian"
  Mise en bouteille au ruisseau.

COME

Come to my senses and get into
my drift.

One of the songs of the mermaids in **comb**. Also given to beckon-
ing with invitations like "Come on over and handle my submerged
company." But don't imagine it was always easy, singing the sailors
to their deaths. Mermaids were known at times to wipe tears from
the drowning men's eyes with their own hair, and dash at their
own cheeks furtively with handkerchiefs pulled out of their vic-
tims' pockets. You could find these handkerchiefs stashed beneath
rocks on the ocean floor as tender mementos of secret regrets and
big wet salty kisses exchanged before the bloating set in.

COUCH

Oh, I love talking with him! He puts all
these couches to lie down on in his sentences.

Yolanta gushing over Jacob's crushing velvet voice and cushy syntax—although on the rare occasion when he'd drag her to a literary
soirée, she often lost him in the crowd. Wending her way among
the "*c'est évident, non?*"s and the "*n'est-ce pas?*"s of frank inter-
course, she'd wind up in a corner stuffing words in edgewise,
batting them against the walls, and making thumbnail sketches
of the *citoyens* inhabiting this crumbling *gâteau*.

CROWN

(from *The Glass Shoe*)

Leaving her crown of thorns with the hat-check girl, she slipped into her carapace and slithered across the parquet floor till she arrived at his pigskin toes.

CUP

Morpheus, in the bottom of this cup of drowsiness, I can see another cup. I knew I was dying of thirst. It's all there, encircled, embraced, how those hours held us and gave us to one another, the room disappearing around us from the moment you came in. I needed to lie still and sleepless beside you, and those final touches, to see you there on that side of the day and in the wide edges between waking and sleep, your hand moving over me, pushing the pillows more closely around me, giving me this extra voluminous body on the sheets almost creamy against my chafed, still stinging skin. I wanted to cry, "Don't leave me! I'll report you for desertion —for abandoning a woman in bed!" as the door opened to the vast terrible daylight swallowing you right out of my arms, and throwing your shadow halfway round the earth. Another time, my love, a hotel with room service, or maybe some snowbound cabin, our frostbitten fingers, extending gracefully from their lustrous knuckles, caressing each other over a salver of Smyrna figs.

"a salver of Smyrna figs"
From Ismir and the land of *Frangipani's Pajamas*, as that traveling shadow attests. Further reading on this shameless fruit in Alexandre Dumas's *Dictionnaire de cuisine*. *Ecco il fico!*

DARK

(from *The Gingerbread Variations*)

Our flesh crept about the room as we
huddled there together in the dark.

Gretl, recounting the ghastly incarceration in that delectable, fra-
grant house—amidst the flashbulbs and brouhaha that greeted the
children's return to their father's shack. She said a lot of stuff that
wasn't true, as long as she had them there eating up her every
word:

> ". . . the ground opened up at these words and we found our-
> selves in a dripping cavern with all sorts of gewgaws hanging
> out of its cracks. But what came after this is so dreadful that it
> would distress me to say any more . . ."

DOLLAR

Stretch your dollar over my body.

Yolanta to some guy, fellow American, in line at the Bureau de Change. Two weeks later found her painting the *salon* and *salle d'entrée* for a French colonel in Boulogne instead, and taking tremendous liberties with the classics in his *bibliothèque*. We can surmise the monologue she delivered to her compatriot—from the last work in which she figured as a dubious, cameo character:

> Yolanta seemed to think that everyone in the world had read "Rameau's Nephew Meets Rappaccini's Daughter"; she referred to it in every conversation she had. This was only one of the signs of her coming dementia (many more were yet to manifest themselves): her delusions became progressively more literary and bizarre.

DOOR

Her door ajar, she came unhinged.

"Her door ajar"
  I don't know what was lurking in the corridor and about to jump her, but the phrase brings to mind both **jar** and the terrors of Timofey, making his comeback in **mirror**. "I left the marble ajar" is how he would put it to himself on his fearful forays after dusk (*"dans les ténèbres,"* the French translation reads), thinking fondly of his nice slab (it was even starting to grow a little moss!) in the cemetery and the smell of resin still clinging to his wooden box, and wishing (for this one night!) he could just stay at home.

⤙ ⤚

"You're distressing my innocence," protested the ingenue of the twinkling breasts and feline haunches as she got past the door of waiting and into the room of womanhood.

"You're distressing"
  After Henry Purcell's *Distressed Innocence Suite*. An earlier aversion begins: "You're distressing my innocence, sweetie." But she was maybe not so sweet or innocent; a later episode in the suite, anyway, says:

> "He pursued her gentle refusal to have a good time with him through an endless corridor of locked doors and pleasant alcoves with rubbings of her earlier *amours*."

⤙ ⤚

. . . then there was this whispery sound,
like an envelope sliding under a door and
over a carpet . . .

(*Note to artist*: Paint a pattern of Oriental carpet that is also somehow the contents of the envelope.)

"Oriental carpet"
   The carpet flew back to its homeland before I could read the
letter and tell you what it said.

                                    ↘ ↖

The molting flamingos crowded around the doorway in
gaping attitudes of incredulity as Torquil and Jonquil stag-
gered out for a postprandial snack two hundred fifty hours
into their acquaintance, which they were eager to further
debauch.

With only four hours to get through, if this is the same place we
last met them, in another book:

> "Their rendezvous at the Last Judgment Pinball Machine
> Motel turned into a 254-hour marathon that neither Torquil
> nor Jonquil would ever regret."

                                    ↘ ↖

Then there was this rapping at the door and many glasses
clattered to the table at once and someone declaimed in broken accents that surely it must be an uninvited guest come to
slaver amongst them and not a messenger of dire tidings to
ruin their revels just yet.

See the **table** of unfinished childhoods.

                                    ↘ ↖

Death, that pickled strumpet, is
just the girl next door.

"*girl next door*"
  Jacob Other in *Eros and Thanatos* traces her development from a
gawky child into a vamp* you'd give your false teeth for a night
with: her pigtails, stuffed animals, and tricycle; the Girl Scout
cookies and braces; the AA-cup bra and first strapless gown, nights
out in backseats of cars.

*In *Frangipani's Pajamas*, we find her as one of the girls in the seraglio with her own tales to tell, of fatal embraces and desperate
cries. Her kinship with the mermaids is also under scrutiny.

DRAWERS

(from *The Glass Shoe*)

No lust lost between me! They were out quaffing Darjeeling and squashing their bustles on overstuffed chairs, so I dropped my dustcloth, sluffed off my rags, and prowled the boudoirs and *salles de bain* to my heart's content, breaking into jars of colors and powders, twirling in petticoats, and giving myself lingering looks in an oval mirror, my amphitheater. I frizzed my bangs, parted my glances, twined my tendrils around my temples, then dumped a few bottles of Veuve Clicquot champagne into a tub of hot water for a bubble bath. Still wet and effervescing I glistened over pieces of furniture, hugging my knees and trying to picture the prince in black pajamas about to slide from his waist. But I didn't get far with this vision, never having seen as much as his face, so I got up and went riffling through drawers sniffing sachets, silk, potpourris, flopped back on a mound of cushions, and I put my finger in that little place where time twitches and spent the rest of the afternoon quietly treacling myself.

Concatenations on the letter *t*, starting with the unmentioned teacups.

DRESS

She was the daughter of a shopkeeper and was married off to a peasant, a downcast peasant with white bread. All her things were carted uphill to his house and she was put in her place. But not for long! She sat for a while on a train beside her husband. He returned to his plowing and sowing and rubbing his roughened hands on his pants. She would go to the beach alone in a long white dress and a big picture hat and watch the waves. She'd watch and wait for a long time in the fog or sun, and when she saw a wild one coming, she'd go out to meet it, and that tumbling suction roaring her under and the way she went with it—that was all she ever lived for.

"She would go to the beach alone"
Once as she came flying along the beach on her bare feet, the big picture hat* sliding back and forth from scapula to scapula, she stubbed one of her toes on a brick** that had certainly, she yelped, hopping about on the other, uninjured foot, not been there the day before when a confusion of currents coming from several directions at once and yet all the while, beneath the surface, not fooling around in the least, but moving *away* from the shore, had nearly dragged her out to sea.

*"The better to see THE BIG PICTURE," she had explained to the milliner who was measuring her head, suggesting a light but durable material, proposing a flattering shape, and a tie so that when she did break into a run crossing the dunes, the hat could jostle around happily over the flaxen hair raveling down to her waist.

**The brick was one of the inert members of the corps de ballet in *The Toes of Nichevo*, the narration in both ballet and radio play accompanied by a band of people brushing their teeth loaned out for the occasions by the producer of *The Telltale Toothbrush*, enjoying a snappy run at a small theater in the West End:

"In the next cottage lived a bricklayer and a woman and another woman," (the narrator continued). "Not what you'd call kept women themselves, they kept his house and kept each other smiling, for he went far to lay his bricks and they often went for weeks with neither hide nor hair of him. So by now he had laid one brick. He tore it out and took it to the beach. There were nine more left to get laid. . . ."

DUSK

In the crepitating dusk of clatters and whispers, he traced each hollow in her candlelit complexion, taking an occasional stab at some veiled meaning that clung to her words as the sea roared on in his *coquilles St. Jacques*.

ESPADRILLES

(from *The Red Shoes*)

Why couldn't she breeze into a room and kick off her espadrilles like other girls? Would she never be able to wash her socks at the village fountain in the morning while the housefronts were being scrubbed, or see her own translucent toenails like seashells in the sun? What must it feel like to slide her soles along fresh white sheets, or to twitch her toes beneath the covers in the afterglow of love?

FACE

I toy with a cup of *café express* on the Place Gambetta, a well-behaved *quartier*, for most of the people who live here are dead. Apollinaire lies in nearby Père Lachaise. Through one of those creepy sensations that are forever crawling over me, I become aware of the stranger at the table next to mine and turn to stare openly at him. As he obligingly or coquettishly turns away his face, I can study his right cheek at my leisure: a poem carved by I know not what sharp and eloquent sort of blade—Burma Shave haiku? It looks like this, but Fenollosa is not available to tell me what it means:

A hearing aid is poised above this very interesting wound, and as I believe it is listening to what I am thinking, I think I had better leave. On the 69 bus from Gambetta to St. Paul, Raymond Queneau's *Exercises in Style* is played by the passengers, for we all take turns treading on each other's toes and uttering mild or serious oaths. I am confronted on this bus with another ideogram carved into the left cheek of an imperious and frowning blonde. But even her frown is not of the moment; someone has left it there:

"study his right cheek"
Running her eyes over whatever reading matter Paris held out to her, Yolanta throwing herself into her unrecompensed work as Paris correspondent for that rambunctious literary review.

FACE

They've been unmasked, and they're
trying to save what faces they have left.

"what faces they have left"
    During the play within a play of **macaroni** where all the
Commedia dell' Arte regulars—Pantalone, Burattino, Grattiano,
Pierrot, Arlecchino, and even Columbine in a suit and Nikes with
pantyhose—are dressed up as bureaucrats in a modern totalitarian
democratic state, several masks at once take turns sliding off one
or another of the actors' faces, and the face-saving grimaces call
for some pretty fast reflexes and snazzy pantomiming through the
rapidly flickering changes on stage. It's a relief for everyone when
the troupe shoves off at last for Pula, its colosseum, and another
engagement, to which Anja had bought tickets weeks in advance
for herself and a gorgeous brute, all six-foot-seven of him, from
Montenegro, actually the sweetest fellow ever to pad through her
house in a dressing gown, and whose incredible mustaches and
revolver no longer caused her the least dismay.

FACE

She greeted him with a sawed-off smile.
He brought her fragile face into focus
and shot her full of questions.

"and shot her full of questions"
   When Yolanta was hauled in to the Préfecture de Police by a
pair of surly *gendarmes* for a little disturbance she had caused on
rue du Roi de Sicile, "they floodlighted her with questions,* and
she blinked in helpless confusion, groping for the switch that
would silence the roaring from that inimical circle of importunate
mouths."

*Things did not get off to a good start with these fellows. She
didn't even bother to answer their preliminary interrogations in
French, replying to *"Votre prénom?"** with "Sweetie, I am Charles
Bukowski trapped in the heart of Emily Dickinson," and so on.

**"Your first name?"

FAREWELL

"Some enchanting evening this has been!" she exclaimed
at her coy hostess, pocketing the rest of the handshake and
seeing herself through the wrought irony gates of the
woman's untoward farewell.

"the rest of the handshake"
    She'd been disagreeable ever since the *métro* station en route,
where a *gamine de clocharde*,* a bottle of *très très ordinaire* wine
sloshing around in *her* ample pocket, had lifted the gloves right off
her hands. See **gloves**.

*A gamine of a tramp.

FEATHER

Torquil, the pink feather that clung to my slipper as one eye opened to the morning and the shoes you were pulling on to walk you away from me: it really *was* pink; it wasn't the rosy fingers of dawn crawling over the carpet. So that claque of flamingos *was* there, their eyes loud with astonishment— or am I anthropomorphizing again?—and it wasn't being famished or delirious making me see things, their fluffy bodies and undulant necks, though I did wonder, afterward, when we returned from that sleazy coffee shop and they were gone.

Jonquil

FEVER

(from *The Red Shoes*)

"And what have you been ingesting, little girl, to bring on
these indecorous metamorphoses?"

Her feet glowed with shame. Oh, wretched radiance! The
doctor wept in his patient's new fuchsia garden. Only the
doctors took her body seriously! His amber bottles glittered
on the floor-to-ceiling shelves, essences of stones, of herbs, of
plagues. He grabbed the hem of her skirt to hold her still, sat
her down, then stroked the arch inside one of the red shoes,
before the needles and further questions, getting closer to the
trouble, farther away from the pain. Her spine arched, her
face curved away, then returned, her eyes steadied themselves
in his as he took her out of them.

"This child is suffering from an early onset of depravity—
an insouciance that so exceeds all possible hidden warmth
that it gives her a feverish glow, a fever that flows in the
dark."

On her way out of Herr Doktor's praxis and this initial consulta-
tion, she encountered a dashing man of handsome middle age limp-
ing into the waiting room humming a few bars from *Der Rosen-
kavalier*, which he'd seen in Vienna the week before. Their visits
with this wizard put them both in high hopes and buoyant spirits:
he bounced out later with a bar of soap in his hand headed for a
double espresso at the Eis-Café Capri, and she could hardly wait to
get back to the hotel and start stimulating her lymphatics! But first
there had been some dark and difficult moments she would never
forget, because while "insouciance" is what the doctor wrote in his
notes to put in her file, what he said to her face was, "I like you
désinvolture," a word with which she was unfamiliar, so it was easy
to hear this as "the design of your vulture" and assume he was trying to tell her in an imagistic way that she had only a few weeks to
live.

FLOOR

(from *The Glass Shoe*)

In the limpid depths and troubled waters of her eyes, he
discerned portents of fiendish devotion, scrubbed floors
and manicured gardens, and not a hint of the adulterous
frivolity nibbling away at her soul. Oh, no, no one would
ever be able to say of *her*, a tumbler of ice cubes melting in
his hand as he turned to a friend and continued with his
story, ". . . then this little mop of a woman came in scooting
across the tiles. . . ."

See sheet **music**, and Cinderella's coloring book its note will
astound you with. Probably a wife-to-be keeping clear of the
corners, à la *Don Juan Is a Woman* wearing **socks**.

FLOUNCES

(from *The Red Shoes*)

She had been a fractious child, but as she grew out of the toy
tea sets and flounces of littlegirlhood, and her honey-colored
hair deepened into a thicker, even richer luster, a sweetness
oozed into her nature and stuck to her every act and gesture
toward the brutes and the frail alike.

FROCK

(from *The Red Shoes*)

She would have loved to drape her stockings over a wild
rosebush, wriggle out of her dirndl,* and plunge into the
swirling waters of a stream, or enjoy the embrace of a passing
wayfarer like any young girl with a soft down on her upper
lip and a generous current of her own streaming through her
eager limbs, but always they were there, the weight, the
clumsiness, even in the ravishment, the heels clacking
together around the waist of her partner as her legs climbed
the air and her voice rose to the heights her pleasure had
reached, just a moment before.

*Yes, dirndls are Austrian frocks, but this girl's great-aunt Elsbeth
had come home from a ski trip in the Tyrol,** and brought back—
half out of pity for the child since she could not get those things
strapped into skis, and if she could, one hates to contemplate the
jeopardy of their dancing over the icy slopes as they pleased, and
half out of the usual great-auntiness that prompts the bearing of
such gifts—a pink-and-white dirndl with silver buttons and bright
blue trim, which she wore in the summertime although it clashed
rather sadly with the scarlet shoes.

**Aunt Elsbeth had gone with a Croatian seamstress named Anja
with whom she had corresponded for five years before their meeting by sending scraps of their work to each other and inspecting
each other's stitchery, exchanging notes on the various problems
each one faced in achieving the flawless buttonhole, collar, or
hem. Elsbeth had spent hours trying to imagine the size and texture
of Anja's hands, the length and condition of her fingernails, while
Anja wondered if she, Elsbeth, laid her work in her lap mostly, or
held it closer to her face, in case she were slightly myopic, or to
give herself better light as it streamed in over her left shoulder.
These were not matters for their correspondence, however, as if at
some point this tacit agreement had been reached, and so their
musings began with and returned to the material world they

shared. The two aging women walked about Innsbruck with their arms around one another's waists, rode narrow-gauge railroads through white alpine tunnels, and flirted with all sorts of men. By day they flew down the slopes in their heavy woolen coats, and by night they rocked the rafters of a succession of dark-timbered lodges with laughter they had saved up for years, for just such an outburst at last as this one, and they parted after three weeks of such behavior like the friskiest of girlhood friends with a lifetime of crooked seams ahead.

F R O C K

Long before Cinderella, her skirt floating about her like
fallen wings,* glided down the stairs from the powder room
to equivocate around the dance floor with the prince and loll
in a corner behind a potted palm catching their runaway
breaths,** the two seamstresses had cut out her wedding
dress, matched it with Valenciennes lace, and were carrying
on a long-distance collaboration over pieces of it, in addition
to the work for their regular customers, Elsbeth trying to keep
her afflicted niece in becoming attire, Anja's cruises, etc. But
when she came to that scene with the orchids and meringue
(see second **toothbrush**), Elsbeth sent a postcard to Anja in
the Dutch West Indies saying, "Hold off on the bodice a
while yet. I have this feeling she may not be going through
with it. I've just done up a jacket of fustian*** for a morose
and ugly man," to which Anja replied, with her habitual
cryptic brevity, "Syntax the Tailor, my dear"—unless it was a
message garbled by the ship's purser in a telegram sent at sea.

*"Why should wings stick out only from shoulder blades?" she
wrote in her diary later that night, remembering how light she had
felt.

**"I told him lots of unlikely stories and waited for my heart to
leap into his mouth."

***I *did* come across a review the other day (in some magazine
with Jacob Other's piece on a poem "New York Boogie-Woogie"
that lays down the rules of a game to play in the painting by
Mondrian) of the pallid author's pastoral prose (see **bodice, gold**).
"Slung together with bits of fustian" is one phrase that leaps to
mind.

FUN

Are you a way to have fun, or
are you just another whack at
being?

She was the sort of girl who would waylay some man she'd never
laid eyes on, happily bearing flowers to the girl he lived with, and
beguile the bouquet right out of his hand, bending his homeward
steps elsewhere—just for the fun of it!

FUR

And this, *this* is winter, this great skinned cat whose
haunches ache and swell with the arthritic vapors curling out
of the Seine, this cat whose whiskers tickle in the pause of
thresholds, and whose consolations are bright and crackling,
the ball of yarn to tangle with over its shuddering, furless
frame.

"the ball of yarn to tangle with over its shuddering, furless frame"
Sounds more like the structure of this book than a description of
winter, if you ask me.

FURBELOWS

How he wished to get past her furbelows, to shorten her
distant gazes, and fill her long pauses with the lowings of
a thousand wanton cows.

As he herded her into his notion of who he thought she was,
the cows ambled aimlessly over his piece of hot property and
beyond the bounds of his beliefs.

GLASS

. . . and so he poured all the most noble of
sentiments into an unfortunately shaped glass.

"into an unfortunately shaped glass"
   From the chapter "Standing Water" in a curious work of nine-
teenth-century decadence comparing love, in all its forms (its
"liquid frameworks"), to this element. Jonquil had doubtlessly read
the book shortly before writing her letter in **rain**.

GLOVES

She sank her slight buttocks onto the bench
with gusto and wiggled into her new kid gloves.

GOLD

Nibbling on an occasional wild berry or the golden meat of a chanterelle on the damp northern island, the emaciated author fashioned lyrical passages out of faraway fragrances while the impostor trampled little lettuces and baby squash blossoms in the fertile soil of her distant empire of a sham Provence.

I'm sorry, but I don't know what this fraudulent-identity nonsense is all about. Why would anyone want to impostor an author? Unless the two of them had some sort of arrangement so that the pale (**bodice**) emaciated author could bang away on her misty island in peace. But why was she pale? The impostor part of this sundered duo is aglow in a radiant sun, and the thumping bodice also makes her an unlikely fill-in for the writer's gaunt bearing, hunched shoulders, and lackluster indifference to food. Apart from these two fragments, there's nothing more about them: nothing pastoral about the prose anywhere else that I can see, and as for the lyricism, well, see Céline in the notes to the Byzantine **T-shirt**. (Hmm. Yeats, too, lived on a damp northern island, with some far-fetched theory about multiple selves, something the hypochondriac was looking into when he got involved with the Theosophists in London.) Is the conjugal bed at the same latitude as the chanterelles? There are no botanical flourishes to the author's side of the story in **bodice**, so maybe she went to the island alone?

HAND

In "The Glass Arachnid," nature enters on eight precise yet broken legs, tracking blood across the page, and it's only after you've turned to the next one that you realize it's not art that bleeds, but your own utilitarian and mutilated hand.

"The Glass Arachnid"
  A review by Jacob Other, a critic of contemporary poetry and prose, and himself the author of two books of poetry, *Winged Sheets* and *The Wronged Number*, both from Echolalia Press. "Wrestling with ideas is my favorite sport," says Jacob, who has a bad back. Hansel and Gretl's witch also had trouble with her back, wrenched in one of her battles against the elements munching away at her form-and-function house. She would soak in the tub, mumbling incantations, and then put ginger compresses over the snarled muscles as she lay on her belly before the hearth upon a rug of—no, I can't tell you what.

HANDKERCHIEF

Morpheus, off hoochy-koochying in someone else's bedroom, apparently, had stood her up three nights in a row. . . .

When Morpheus finally did show up, as if nothing had happened, as if he hadn't left her alone night after night, to flatten her body out over the mattress like a starfish, digging her nails into its sides, she gave way to a tirade of bitter reproaches, jealous rantings, the tears of an abandoned child, and only after he took her into his arms and murmured her name and some smutty endearments did she fall into a heavy, exhausted slumber like a soaked and twisted handkerchief.

HANDS

(from *The Gingerbread Variations*)

She was starved for company, and especially adored little
visitors in short pants and wool jumpers stumbling through
her neck of the woods in a famished condition and holding
consanguine hands.

HANDS

(from *The Little Match Girl*)

I struggled out with my *allumettes* and blew through the snow
from door to door dressed in my fur cap and hands. I ought to
explain about the hands. They were stitched together and
wrapped about my throat and tossed over my left shoulder
with some fingers pointing down my back. I could not afford
a professional manicure, but the nails, well kept, and polished with Alabastro, gleamed in the moonlight thrown at
them from the dazzling swath I cut in my reindeer boots.

It was Noël, and I passed many windows stuffed with
patresfamilias displaying their generous sides before fireplaces
in which silver paper occasionally flared, or a green ribbon,
over logs from our northern forests, of pine, of spruce, of fir.
My nostrils flared in forgetful pleasure as I passed through
zones of various smokes blending in ever different combina-
tions and here and there paused to sniff deeply of them.

Then I came to a large window that returned me to my
other senses, and I remembered as I looked through it at the
swollen movements of grandmothers being indulgent and the
smug contentment of three generations all feasting at once
about the cold piercing my bones and my wretched blanket
in a corner at home where we were lucky to burn coal if there
were anything to burn, let alone eat, at all, and how I
couldn't even go back there for shelter if not warmth without
selling the matches. My own hands were cold because they
were bare and wrapped around my tray of matches in such a
way that I couldn't dig them into my cuffs and keep a grip on
the merchandise. I may sound rather blasé about this now,
but I was growing more bitter and frozen at each step that
returned me always to this same window no matter which
direction I attempted to follow, and I had to keep cajoling

myself out of the snowdrifts of self-pity I kept sliding into,
which is easy when there's no one to talk to, and you're half-
crazed from hunger and not quite numb enough for oblivion.
Had one door that night been opened to me in the most
tentative of gestures, I would not have hesitated just because
I looked a fright and my manners were only half polished
from what I'd learned by watching through windows of other
houses like this one on spring evenings in drawing rooms.
Christmas forgives all shortcomings, accepts the chipped
tooth, the little asymmetries that make each of us who we
are, perfect in the very arrangement of aberrations by which
we embody the hope and teleology of the human form.

"the dazzling swath I cut in my reindeer boots"
    Someone else was responsible for her wardrobe in Renoir's *La
Petite marchande aux allumettes.* An officer on his way to his wassails
pauses to size up the situation and her feet, saying, "With shoes
like those you'd be better off at home."
    A more ardent lover come to court *la petite** arrives on a
deserted stage set shortly thereafter to announce: "I have an
appointment with Karen tonight. I am DEATH!"

*Nowhere in this film does he or anyone else break into song with:

> *Allumetta, gentille Allumetta,*
> *Allumetta, je te fumerai.*
> *Je te brûlerai les fesses,*
> *Je te brûlerai les fesses.*
> *Allumette! Allumette! Oh!*

HAT

DEATH IN VENICE HAT

She bought a black velvet hat and chased a
little boy in a sailor suit all over town.
When she wanted to sleep the *signore* would
then appear and row her straight out to sea,
a tropical disease.

HONEY

Morpheus, you came to me last night wearing earrings and you bangled into bed with shiny skin like a dark lady gleaming with secret siestas, a thousand and one tricks up her stockings, and something else to be taken, not given, and not for her to decide. I pulled you to me, pawing your breasts that rose in my hands like bread made of honey and the finest durum wheat, and you moaned and rolled over so I could admire your back shuddering each kiss I tasted of it, coming before you could wonder what the world was coming to as it came to meet you with each pulsing, answered plea. I wrapped you in my nightgown, the one you tore once twisting me out of it, just a slash along the hole my arm reached out from to get at you, and held your head in my lap in the turn it now was mine to sing you to sleep in this dark night of our body reversed. My little girl, visions of sugar daddies dancing in her head, my little paloma, my big woman of a jukebox at rest. You arrived in a cloud of smoke, damp and glowing, and the faces you showed me kept waking me through the late-mooning hours, so that by dawn I was discursing on them, finally finding the dream tongue to speak the cat had made off with into the shadowed walls you brought down. My hand, soaked in your colors, reached for you when I awoke at noon, nothing but a strand of long black hair on the pillow to tell me the truth. Later, in red shorts and shiny legs, someone who seemed to have escaped one of those faces to haunt my waking, smearing her lips and slicking down her hair on the way to the elevator we shared. Darling, I know you're out there, in bright daylight, beads of moisture on your mother-of-pearly upper lip, your hips so slightly swinging as you cast your eyes down shyly and ask, "Breasts, where are you going?" and their silence sounds the roundness off the dress I can't catch you in.

Although obviously one of the *Sonnets to Morpheus*—which are not sonnets at all, and are an insult to Rilke, as well as to his many fine translators, viz. Stephen Mitchell and Edward Snow—this piece seems to be also part of another work, *The Troubled Succubus*.

"of the finest durum wheat"
    More often found in pasta, but this is such a tangled mess of mixed metaphor that it's not really so out of place.

HOTEL

I fled headlong into the unknown man.
His navel is my hotel.

"His navel is my hotel"
    Which must be the place, and not the frayed **pockets** of silken misery, Yolanta is thinking of when she writes elsewhere in her notebooks: "I love my little hotel."

HOUSE

(from *The Gingerbread Variations*)

Aren't you wondering how she baked her gingerbread house?
It's such a grotesque process that I don't want to frighten you
with all the details, but I will tell you this much: she cooked
it with her own body. And she could get quite mawkish
about her own childhood while she was tampering with the
oven's thermostat or shoving one of the youngsters through
its see-through door.

JAR

He conducted a William Carlos Williams tour of her soul,
fingering the implements in her kitchen cupboards, rattling
her cake pans, imploring her jelly molds, pushing her around
in her red wheelbarrow, and holding in a certain light her
jar, which was not in Tennessee.

"in her red wheelbarrow"
    Yolanta, during her "no ideas but in things" phase. The jar,
which was empty, contained all her notions of "home." Sitting
there on its American windowsill, it became the focus of Yolanta's
nostalgia, and the object (recipient? receptacle?) of numerous
yearning postcards over those years she spent abroad.

KIMONO

Morpheus, the nights are breaking over me, like your body
demanding mine, but it goes on, this voice of a voracious
woman, whether or not you're here to listen, to yell, "Stop
thrashing around!" while holding me down, or "Stop bleating!" as the wool catches on fences between me and sleep
and I collect it to make blankets for all the women and children of the world twitching with fears and desire. It always
feels like I'm trying on your love, so no wonder you sent me
the kimono, like slinking into something, and sometimes I
can't tell if I'm putting it on or taking it off, the way it is
with any truly agreeable garment, somehow better than nothing at all: how you enwrapture me! These thicknesses passing
over and pressing through me, the denseness and lightness
floating and sinking, and us: a stranger I keep becoming a
part of, unsure of how much of myself to pour into it, how
much of you to mix with, assuring myself that I can get
through anything alone, even get through being with you.
But of course I will never get away with that, and you got
away with me this morning before I could hold on to a last
sensation of you, a promise you'll be there again.

KISS

What're you doing—cleansing my palate?

See note to second **lunch,** not the one with crumbs of kulebyaka scattered over the table and leftover grechaniki and onions.

LAP

Torquil, I'd say I was surprised to hear from you, but I
thought I passed you on the street the other day, so I figured
you'd be showing up. We were in Paris, and we both skirted
opposite edges of an open manhole. There was a unicorn at
the bottom of it, waiting for a virgin to lay her head in its
lap. But no virgin came (though they sometimes do), and this
unicorn was battering its horn. No wonder we swayed across
the street ensemble, darling, ensemble, between headlights,
horizons, coffee, and dessert.

Jonquil

"between headlights, horizons, coffee, and dessert"
   In those trysts with Torquil, coffee acted as an aphrodisiac for
Jonquil, and thus acquired the mystique of rite and symbol in
which her clamoring cup rejoiced. The drink appears in every allusion she makes to her lover, so that even the cooling of her passion
for him is expressed in terms a Costa Rican economist would *con
mucho gusto* comprehend:

> I awoke in the snow at the
> bottom of the coffeepot.

LAVALAVA

(from *The Little Match Girl*)

Teeth of winter, sinking into my flesh, my own clacking
against each other like knitting needles, and I wish they'd
knit a heavy shawl around my shoulders before widening into
a yawn. Why do I always yawn when I'm cold? I think of the
star that's a frozen toe tossed into the sky by Thor. If only . . .
the only teeth clacking were the ones slung with shells
around my neck and tossing to and fro, biting at the torpid
sunbeams of a Gauguin afternoon, luscious, frothy, I could
eat that sky with a spoon. Like one of those tropical cocktails
that have such vulgar names, juices of mango, guava, passion
fruit dribble down my chin, plashing onto my belly as I undu-
late in my lavalava with a flamingo on a leash. My tangled
hair, streaked with salt and sunlight, damp with sweat, se-
men, fructose, is plastered to my shoulder blades and clings to
my bouncing breasts, my navel crusty with submarine miner-
als from a recent plunge in the sea. Among our legs, the
flamingo's and mine, entwine our lovers of various sexes and
species, with iridescent insects crawling across their overlap-
ping furs, feathers, and skins, a drum in the distance setting
up its beat in my heart. The flamingo molting in our mingled
footprints, I am drenched, brimming, my fur hands, stripped
and pink, coaxing one of the nearby bodies into a state of
arousal while I sink onto my knees and sear his senses with
the flames licking out of my fingertips as I light another
match and cup its warmth to my face.

LEER

(from *The Glass Shoe*)

"And whose womb did you wamble out of, little girl?" leered a rheumatic marmaduke, breathing deeply on his lorgnette, polishing it off, and scrutinizing my porcelain cheeks.

"a rheumatic marmaduke"
   Lorgnette and all restraint cast aside, a duke who had eaten too freely of Yolanta's toast and marmalade before popping up at the ball.

It took Cinderella a fortnight to record her many impressions, panoramic and pointillist, of the ball—and that's *nothing* compared to Anja's months of pawing through splintered portraits and reportage to sort out which face belongs with which body, let alone whom the ensemble was dancing or flirting with, or trying to evade or pursue, and what was said to or thought of whom, and at what critical moment the prince's big foot came down with a terrible pressure and show-stopping tinkle upon the handle-with-care glass shoe.

L E G S

Effie and the catty little clique of nymphs she ran around with would gather in the afternoon shadows of laurel and cypress, giggling over their hot and panting pursuers, gob-bling confections of rose water and walnuts, and waxing each other's legs.

The faun, fagged out and disgusted after five years of Effie's evasions among the Mediterranean flora, took up with a Teuton named Hilda and departed for her home in the Schwarzwald in a silver Mercedes Benz.

"hot and panting"
  Close in feeling is Yolanta's review in *Passion* of a poetry reading she rated, as a pick-up joint, Hot to Trot:

> "It was a good chance to mince about on bruised forelegs among ungulate brethren pricking forward ears of augmented attention to the beckoning snorts of randy mares."

LIGHT

She couldn't tell whether the paper she held in her hand was blue or green. She had to be absolutely sure. Green she could never send. There wasn't a single light in the house she could trust.

"Green she could never send"
    See also the somnolent, refrigerated ponies in **salt**. The color appears again in Yolanta's alliterative rendering of the backdrop in *The Toes of Nichevo:**

      Alone asking no greenness nor gardens   no
      antelopes no ancestors Alone we dance

*Nichevo is the beer-drinking neuter pronoun tracking water into the footnote of **towel**.

LIPS

As she sawed into the parchment in which her *saumon aux roses fumées* had been baked, several random phrases (something about a tin goat and an Albanian losing his way) caught his incredulous eye across the table, but before he could raise his eyebrows to the level of astonishment he did in fact feel, she had lifted the toasted page to her lips and swallowed it, and all was lost once again.

Every sentence that fell from her lips was some sort of cliffhanger, or else a proverb in partita form—and now this! With her food!

The night was not yet embroidered with sequins. In fact, the evening has not worn on much further than where we left this couple in **dusk**.

"an Albanian"
    This evanescent and woebegone wanderer was a key figure in the attachment Anja (of **frock**) so precipitately formed for the tailor's dummy on the ship. Tatters of *The Secret of the Lost Albanian* kept popping up in the stories her Aunt Milanka had embroidered her childhood with—and here, years and life stories later, a chance encounter with an attractive speechless stranger at sea was delivering some of the original manuscript (long lost) into her own needleworking hands. Read **scar** very *soon*. It was thus that Anja determined to bundle the dummy back to Istria—and became the mastermind of the book now held in *your* hands.

LUNCH

About this week's meeting of the Slavic Gastronomes: You
forgot to eat the caviar I forgot to offer you. You also missed
Boris, in fine form and offering me "a piece of coffee," on a
Russian poet who remains in a dark room in Minsk: "He has
his cup of dirt in that life there."

Next week will be at Bougival, outside the gates of
Turgenev's dacha and birch trees overlooking the Seine.

Menu (*prix fixe*): Vasko's Popovers, Alexander's Pushovers,
                  Crimean Punishments, and Dead Soles
                  And some torrents of spring in a carafe
                                       Yolantska Pavelovna

"*at Bougival*"
    After a slight detour into the unappetizing but brilliant story
"The Rat Catcher," by Alexander Grinevski, or Grin, they went on
to discuss narration in the later Russian writers, and clinked their
glasses of vodka* in total agreement that the real masterpieces
were written in either the first person peculiar or the third person
deranged. This goes for chaps like Kuprin and Olesha as well as the
better-known dog** and madman of Gogol's little gem.

*Little realizing that in so doing they were coming perilously close
to falling into the blini woman's borscht (**babushka**).

**"The style is very jerky. You can see that it's not written by
a man. She starts off all right and then lapses into dogginess."
                                        —*The Diary of a Madman*

LUNCH

She was so hungry for knowledge
she ate a professor for lunch.

Probably the same graduate student* or avid scholar in this sequence from *Carnal Knowledge*, its pursuit after dark:

> She spent the evening dodging the captious interjections of
> an educated imbecile bent on hauling her off to his bed in a
> riptide of her own sapience gone astray.

> The minute he touched her she started lucubrating.

*If it *was* the graduate student, then at least the first of these is
about her. The epigraph to her philosophy dissertation says:

> If there's something more to know,
> I don't want to.

MACARONI

They have their antics.
They cavort about the plate of macaroni.
Quips and antics follow.
The magician weaves a few incantations and the
satyr is transformed into an emancipated woman.
He shambles into the grotto.
The nymph scrapes some lichen off the trees
and attempts to plaster it to her body.
They organize a holiday in Istria and set off
across the Adriatic with much further *adieux*.

MAD

She walked in and started battering him
with this HUGE VOICE.

"and started battering him"
  From *The Battering Bride*, a ballet the girl in red shoes (and oh,
they felt heavy that night! especially during *Tulle Eulenspiegel's
Merry Pranks*) attended while careening through Bohemia to
Gottwaldov, where the curator at the Museum of Shoes awaited
her with a covetousness quite overshadowing the purely professional curiosity his letter had expressed.

MIRROR

Timofey trembled. His terror was beginning once again.
Night was daubing at the twilight, closing in on the world
about him and crushing his spirits. No comfort at all that he
was a spirit himself! He scratched his head with his ghost
limb, knowing, and it was a dreadful knowledge, that he
would soon have to go out into the street.

Nadia was polishing her nails. Her curtains were open,
letting the soft night air in on her face, a chiaroscuro caress,
considering the light bouncing off the glass. She felt something stirring in the air apart from that erotic crepuscular
breath, a menace she could not put her finger on, a horror
she could not name. She felt something rise within her, a
longing, a cry, yet her body remained rigid, holding itself
onto the moment as something toppled inside her and broke.
At the same time she heard a soft crash like a fingernail falling through the branches of the tree outside her yawning
curtains. She stiffened, closing her hand around the bottle
on the table before which she sat. In the mirror, her face,
and another face behind it, less opaque than hers. Both faces
wore startled expressions of speechlessness with gaping
mouths and sundered lips. He was back! Timofey! His hands
were on her neck, lightly poised along the veins. His unmis-
takable touch. Nadia's cleavage heaved quietly as in the days
when there had been flesh on these fingers which were now
of a creepy diaphanous substance, and smelling of subterra-
nean depths.

Timofey *was* speechless. He was busy reading her thoughts.
They read like a cheap tabloid and he was wishing he'd never
come. His hands wandered farther down over her marble
breasts. She was every bit as cold as he had been these last
two years underground. This life had no more to offer him
than the nebulous realm in which he had been ambling,

bumping into other shades and having cozy little chats! he gathered, and he left the way he had come. He did not look back at her as he departed. And she had eyes only for herself.

A chapter from *Tidings of Timofey*, a Russian ghost story about a specter afraid of the dark. The literary chatter at the Slavic Gastronomes' **lunch** never sank to this level of tawdry entertainment.

"polishing her nails"
 The color was Afterwards Verbena, one of a dozen bottles of Emily Dickinson nail lacquers she had recently purchased from a wandering minstrel and cosmetics salesman.* Nadia had just rubbed off some chipped and outgrown The Rose Is Out of Town, and had deliberated as the sun was setting among Interrogate the Daisies, Later the Peach, and Shrill Felicity before settling on this not too gaudy pink.

*Cinderella, too, had received this peddler on her doorstep, and squandered household money earmarked for a *tapénade* on a bottle of perfume, also of the Emily D. collection, "avouched to rouse the slumbering beast in even the most benumbed or befuddled bridegroom," called Sweet Wolf Within. She went on to promise that if he'd pass by again, she'd buy a foot cream that quite tickled her fancy—Doom's Electric Moccasin.

MOOD

(from *The Glass Shoe*)

The prince wore a jacket that looked like ironed milk, but I
was in a wrinkled linen mood. My mouth was full of easy
vowels and lagging answers, and I stared long into my demi-
tasse after finishing off a Turkish coffee: women's bodies
brimming with child, mountains shaggy with fur. I don't
want to end up as one of those women who cry themselves to
sleep at night over a mismatched life. The prince is very nice,
not at all standoffish or anything; his crown has obviously
not gone to his head, and even though he's an only child
raised with a silver spoon in his nanny's right hand, and
tutors in German, Greek, Italian, English, Russian, and
French lisping and spluttering and sibilating at his elbow,
and has had little girls all over the realm falling at his dashing feet from the day he stopped crawling, I find him kind,
considerate, capable of crossing over into a woman's feelings
and anticipating and fulfilling her needs before she even
knows what they are herself . . . and yet I never break into
slivers of astonishment over the fact that there he is, beside
me, in all his fine skin and raiment, at once annihilating me,
the *éclat* of his presence bringing me crashing to the floor like
the vase I broke the other day as I was dusting around the
M's in the library (Maugham, Monrós, Marias), and then
scooping me up and completing me in the very depths of my
demise. Oh, sure, he's a good dancer, and can converse on
any number of trivial or serious matters, keeping the corners
of my lips curled with amusement or my forehead crinkled in
concentration, but when I come home and shrug off my
clothes and tuck myself in between my own familiar humble
covers, I am ravaged with ennui, and start chewing on the
sheets. Perhaps something has been bred out of this boy. So I

thought the other day, wondering where is the ache my heart desires:

> And what manner of beast might you once have been? A hideous creature has been enchanted and turned into a shiny prince. Its only wish: to get back its horns and scabs and slink back into the muck whence it was wrenched.

My elastic good fortune, snapping me in the face.

"like ironed milk"
   She drones on with a recitative of her responsibilities for "this gaggle of females called home" in the letter to her father that twines and whines through the diary:

> "And then, after I've got a healthy roar going in the fireplace and have dropped several knives on my feet, I have to put out the milk bottles and rub down the front steps.* It's astonishing how much milk this household goes through in a single typical day, but they do lower their splendid abundances into bathtubs of it and splash and purr like kittens, sop up saucers of the stuff with Café Noir cookies and honeybuns at tea, and after dinner souse apple tarts or pear-and-apricot cobblers** in clabbered milk—their idea of a just dessert. It really is too bad you didn't stick around long enough to enjoy your own daughter's culinary talents in bloom!"

*In other moods on two unconnected days, the steps take part in a metaphoric descent—"Down the steps of consternation!"—and become the subject of grisly speculation: "I have often wondered if this bejowled old broad*** is called my stepmother because my real mother is buried beneath the steps, and we have to step over her to get into the house."

**Not the same cobbler who distracted Red Shoes from her torments, although he *is* referred to in one passage as "a rustic *délice* smelling of leather and plum trees," an allusion to his bottle of Slivovitz.

***What a rich store of description the diary leaves us with! There's this semiprecious glimpse of the ugly stepmother at the ball; as you will notice, Cinderella had sobriquets of her own:

> "And there was Mamaliga, her jowls wagging back and forth, rhinestone earrings like bawdy chips off fallen stars slapping the aspic flesh while she boogied and batted her eyelashes at a gouty pharmacist."

"in between my own familiar humble covers"
The covers of this book.

MOON

Her face brushes across a surrendering sea.
"Call me in the evening," she says, "my
appointment book is on fire."

"my appointment book is on fire"
    Her lunarcyclical schedule of rendezvous may have found its way
(after the mugging on rue du Roi de Sicile, note to the fragile **face**)
into Yolanta's electrical appliance heating up in note to **bread**.

MOUTH

Morpheus, I do keep wondering about these scratchmarks
crossing over from those hands I know, talking to me like
that, just asking for questions burning in the mouth of every
answer I haven't given you yet.

"just asking for questions"
    In the mock dialogue of *Carnal Knowledge*, where love triumphs
over a reductio ad absurdum and is at one point reviled as "nothing
more than the philosophical consequence of the body's arguments,"
we find:

> "Because, you gorgeous dingbat, you don't belong in the
> mouth of every question ever posed."

Cf. the ingenue at the distressing threshold of **door**: "Hey, I don't
go around jumping into just anybody's mouth!"

MUD

Her tongue scalded from the cup of cocoa and her mind filled
with terrors of the tale she had just laid aside, she tossed fit-
fully among the bedclothes while mummies masquerading as
hieroglyphs packed her, lace nightie and all, into the silt of
the riverbank and spelled out her destiny in an awkward per-
formance of calisthenics as her eyes peeped in fright from the
mud.

The contents of this nightmare are understandable if one assumes
that the tale she'd been disturbing herself with was "The Mauled
Scribe."

M U G

He drank deeply of her mug
of reconciliation.

"deeply of her mug"
    Because he and she were twin souls, and suffered one another's
admiration with mixed feelings, there was a Russian proverb*—
"Do not chafe at the looking glass if your mug is awry"—she was
fond of quoting when he mistook some ambiguous arrangement of
her features and skulked off to her boudoir to ponder the surfaces
of his own.

*Never one to repeat herself, she varied this with as much inven-
tion as she could muster, producing improvisations such as:

> "Do not spit in your mind's eye while gargling the
> malentendus of yesteryear";

> *"Fais pas la gueule devant la vitrine où se reposent les sous-
> vêtements de votre belle-mère"***;

and once, while waxing her own mustache,

> "Quaver not before your mirror lisping, 'You're gorgeous,'
> fingering your lips, your greased moon of a face, tasting glass
> as your tongue laps reflection of rouge and jaw, if they are
> streaked with tears."

**"Don't make faces in front of a display window where your
mother-in-law's underwear is sleeping."

MUG

Grüss Gott! At the Eis-Café in Baden-Baden, where my
blond sylphic immensity feels slightly more at home than the
last place you heard me from. My cup runneth over with
essentials (just cashed a traveler's check), and my mug is
frothing over with excitement: I'm fresh from snow falling
into gushing bowls of radioactive waters among *somnambules*
of various large red sizes bobbing up and down and sinking
further into flesh—the same ones who might be seen here
morning or afternoon spooning foam into mouths beneath fur
hats or newspapers and the frown of the German soul which
seems to be saying, "There's no rest for the wicked, *und* zoo
feeling *arbeiter* for the good." On the wall, four girls, seasonal
tableaux, tilt their bosoms over the four gentlemen, at their
separate tables, digging into *Schlag* and dragging on cigarettes. Autumn's belly opens beneath pumpkin breasts;
Spring, in pale green gossamer, squats in a field of Neapolitan
blooms—pink petals edged with chocolate and white—and
surrounds one branch with her thighs, pulls another to her
lips. Must go see if I can replace the little strip of leather that
broke off my boot yesterday on the hotel stairway and was
carried off by the Park-Villa bulldog, whose paws have more
than once found my handknit skirt. Ah, these carbonated
muscles, this tingling, fizzing skin! *Das ist alles—alles für
nichts*, if there's no letter from you in Paris in a few weeks.
                                                        Yolanta

"*my cup runneth over*"
   Somewhat more prosperous than during "my *Les Misérables*
times," Yolanta was not in Baden-Baden to lose her royalties at the
blackjack tables of its opulent casino, but to consult a physician of
extraordinary intuitive powers about "a commotion in my discon-
nective tissue," and to take the famous cure.

"my handknit skirt"

It *was* a fetching little number an editor in New York had sent her two days after lunch at a French bistro called Tout-Va-Bien, where things went well enough through the steamed mussels and crème caramel once he'd poured a glass of white wine into her lap while pulling out her chair. But chic she was not (see **pajamas**), and as for all those things they were saying about her—"Fictions, my dear—mummery tissue," as she dismissed them in one interview.

MUSIC

He at last found out she was a piece
of sheet music anyone could play.

"a piece of sheet music"
    That unhappy discovery was not made in Jacob Other's *Winged Sheets*, but is a caption in a coloring book* of Cinderella's called *Loose Women and Tight Corners*, a take-off on *Little Women and Bright Corners*, which had been a manual for new brides in her mother's day on the way to a man's heart ("go straight for fifty years and then take a turn for the worse") and "brightening the corner and staying there."

*This coloring book of women with two heads and double lives, their garments awrithe with ribbons to color in somber and scandalous shades, is the only thing our girl ever shoplifted (she slipped it beneath her camisole) in all those days of haggling, snapping green beans, sniffing melons, and sticking out her tongue so the Armenian cheese man could lay slivers of Kasseri, Mimolette, and Provolone upon it and feast his eyes on the felicities invading her features while his wife in the back room lifted crates and moaned.

MUSIC

(from *Peter Quince at the Clavicles*)

He pounded upon her ill-tempered clavicles
with a bacchanalian bravado that calmed his
seething soul.

"with a . . . bravado"
  A bra worn by a bullfighter. When she had first met him, she
spoke ardently of "that flagging, bright, rustling bravado he has,"
and fingered her own lingerie with fresh disdain.
  In *Frangipani's Pajamas*, Armada and Flotilla spend an uproar-
ious afternoon in a Barcelona boutique trying on knickers and
bravados.

NIGHTGOWN

He was awakened at the creak of dawn by a flannel flapping
sound. Although it had no knees to speak of, a long-sleeved
nightgown with rows of roses climbing blue-and-white lat-
tices knelt in the doorway waving its lace-cuffed arms and
swaying from side to side to a rhythm he couldn't quite put
his finger on, but which smacked of Africa.

As he soon discovered, the flannel nightgown was in fact a
gospel singer, and regaled him with its sabbath repertoire
until the first rays of daylight broke in on the shadows of that
full-bodied voice, which disappeared into a laundry chute.
This gave his silk dressing gown something to think about
after he'd slammed the door on his breakfast of solitude and
caught the tramway of travail. What sweet emotions those
folds of flannel had evoked! No matter that the hands that
might have been clapping were now rubbing the contralto
over the washboard as its mouth filled up with soap and the
Hallelujahs caused large bubbles to burst in the sun. The silk
dressing gown, which had never been immersed in such stuff
in its life, nor submitted to an abrasive touch on its fine and
many-colored threads, made sure the coast was clear before
stepping into the hallway and entering a new life before the
mirror of gyrations and fervor theretofore in its murkiest
dreams unspun.

Another instance of the sort of thing not to be missed in doorways,
as a glance through any **door** should show.

"*disappeared into a laundry chute*"
    This can't be the same laundry room we will encounter in the
note to that last and watchful **time**, Timofey's *remorse*—a nether-
world where the nightgown, belching Allelujahs, would appear an
unseemly guest. Although, come to think of it, that couple strip-
ping beside the basement washers and dryers in **undershirt** . . .

PAIN

Would the endorphins *never* come?

PAJAMAS

Bon giorno!

Your letter tracked me down at the American Express in Rome, a city they seem to be giving back to the wolves (well, I was propositioned only three times today between my morning cappuccino and lunch, over which I am dawdling, the polenta with octopus all inky like this note, and far from home, like me). Rumors reaching me that my last book was said to have been written by "a chic lesbian living in Rome," I decided I'd avoided this part of Italy too long, and swerved down here through Orvieto and a night on a floor above a hillside village bakery because a baby had arrived to occupy the guest room I'd been offered two years before. I see you are learning to make ideas take off their pajamas, and that's one way of getting at the naked truth. I've been undressing the authors who hide in me, but so far have unearthed no Albert Camus. Here comes *il addizione.* And an espressoed kiss.

Yolanta

PANTS

Still in the Marais, whose streets are as dark and closed as this December. I notice that in German, my multilingual corduroy pants, made in Scotland but thrown out at me by someone in London before they got to the jumble sale, are made of *Baumwolle*—tree wool. Upstairs in the hotel, the Panamaniac's library is being built, and all his books, transported from Spain, are covered with fluffs of dust called *moutons*—sheep (did they pick these up crossing the Pyrenees?). Books being made of trees, sheep coming to rest on books, forests sprouting fleece, I conclude that my lower garments deserve further study. My hands read the lines in corduroy curving over my thighs, and a mutual understanding is reached.

"read the lines in corduroy"
    See the Yolanta note to **face** where she's perusing a storylined cheek.

PELISSE

As the pelisse slid from her generous shoulders and tumbled
onto the tumulus of wraps on the bed—cloaks, fur coats,
capes (she noticed a red one a bit shredded around the
hood)—she caught sight of a small figure flickering at the
window through the frosted pane, and her hand reached to
rearrange the warm jewels at her throat, just like Saint
Agnes' Eve, she thought, wondering of whom she would
dream in the coming dawn, and at the rough little beast outside.

"*rough little beast*"
    Obviously the little match girl at the window, growing shaggier
by the minute in her tango with the wolf, her teeth tearing at her
own flesh, the fur hands sharpening their nails. But the pelisse
itself was a *modèle* called "Slouching toward Bethlehem," as the
label sewn to its furry lining read.

PERFUME

PARFUM DES DEUX MAGOTS

Because her existence *was* her essence, he reduced her to it
and bottled it and wore it splashed, with studied casualness,
over his anomie as he dragged the boulevards.

PETTICOATS

(from *The Glass Shoe*)

In the year 186—, Miss A— was just beginning to become aware of a number of new, though not entirely unpleasant, sensations in the region enlaced by her petticoats, somewhere between her navel and her knees. . . .

"Miss A—"
    A pale outline of a figure in *Loose Women and Tight Corners*.* Cinders dusted her cheeks with ashes and Nature Morte Blusher to suffuse them with the quiet commotion the escapades on the ensuing pages richly rewarded and amplified.

*The enormous success this coloring book had—in such far-flung places as Constantinople, where it scored as big a hit with the eunuchs as with their fluttering charges, and a clinic in Switzerland, whose director found therapeutic applications for its games among his malaised matrons—led to a sequel called *Loose Women in Tight Clothing*, with a mail-order catalogue of garb attached, and undersizing advice offered for its wet T-shirts and constricting nighties to crawl out of the minute chance came crashing through the shrubbery and bashing down one's door.**

**The last bit of this sentence was stolen from *Sleepless Beauty*, about a loquacious insomniac, as were the so-called *Sonnets to Morpheus*, mere previews of the *accouchements* to come.

PIZZA

I was in a Chinese restaurant.
Everyone was eating pizza.

One of Yolanta's alienation dreams, from the same rough time, or
roughly the same time, as her "La dame aux échecs"* phase:

> Dream of my life as a chess game. Each time a piece moves
> into a new square, it mutters, " Oh, shit!" or "*Merde!*"

*_Échecs:_ chess or failures.

PLACE

Aimless wandering can lead directly to a kind of roughhouse.
It is a large, sprawling, boisterous, and absolutely wonderful
place. This repulses many people seeking an easier way to
their sandwiches.

"a kind of roughhouse"
The tavern a day's eastward journey from Plzeń you will arrive in
shortly without your fairy tale T-shirt was also very noisy, with so
many different native tongues loosened by every alcoholic concoc-
tion dreamed up on either side of the Danube flapping at once; and
served no sandwiches, but meat, cabbages, potatoes, paprika, and
onions combined in more ways than seems possible to our jaded
palates. The blind innkeeper Frantisek, an autodidactic polyglot,
stood around jawing with the customers while his formidable wife
Katja, a woman of phenomenal constitution and mandibles, ran
the whole show, giving birth at dawn to one baby after another till
they numbered thirteen, slaughtering oxen in the noontime sun,
dealing with the peasants who supplied what food they didn't raise
themselves, supervising the airing of the linens from the second-
story windows, keeping an eye out for pickpockets in the smoky
den of iniquity the hostel might at any moment become, and still
found the time, energy, and maternal instinct to tell the bashful
servant girl to take her fingers out of her mouth.

PLACE

(from *The Gingerbread Variations*)

ARRIVAL FOR FOUR VOICES:

I think we're in the wrong place.
I'm just glad we found it.
I hope we never leave.
Maybe we could take it with us.

"Arrival for Four Voices"
   Four lost children at first sight of the gingerbread house while
straying through the woods. There are many fugues of similar
theme in the gingerbread archives (not part of the *Lebkuchen-
häuschen* canon proper), thanks to the tapes that were confiscated
when the witch was burned. A true artist at heart, she had embed-
ded a voice-activated cassette recorder in a patch of gumdrops
embellishing the front gate so that she could later play back these
comments of passersby and captivated little ones, take note, then
give them serious consideration as she made her sketches for re-
doing the cake in the spring.

POCKETS

Whenever she cooked dinner, she kept
her apron pockets stuffed with caramels
made of little sayings of Emily Dickinson.

Stuffing her skirt into its own
pockets, she looked for something
to hide.

She pocketed the change
hoping everything would
remain the same.

No, I won't live in your pocket.
It's too dark down there, and
I'd always be slapping your thigh.

He told me to keep in touch
so I chopped off his finger
to carry in my pocket.

She worked her way into his
pocket, looking for a short
cut to take him by surprise.

There was once a little girl
who had a little pocket
right in the middle of her
thighs.

"once a little girl"
    Mistakenly identified by Jacob Other as a nursery rhyme from
Guillaume des Forêts' *Trois oies dans une babushka,* this is actually
a translation back into English of a chapter in *La Vie in the Wild
Forest* by Danielle Mémoire, whose admirable *Le Biscuit inachevé*
is on its way out of the ovens at Pantagruel Press.

POCKETS

She broke out in a case of small
pockets and a cholera of fur.

"a cholera of fur"
    When she slunk her nappy eminence into the Schwarzwald
doctor's praxis for a third visit, he carefully avoided encouraging
false expectations of ever shedding this strange growth she found
rather cozy through the first blustery winter, but an encumbrance
and embarrassment at Bayreuth the following July. "You're just
banging your fur head against the wall,"* he told the girl straight
out with kindness but no mercy, stroking a shaggy forearm and
making a mental note to put something in her file about the
healthy sheen this pelt had recently acquired.
    The small pockets also brought a swarm of new troubles, a mot-
ley procession of beggars trailing after her wherever she went. On
an Istrian holiday, and exasperated by the local mendicants' atten-
tions, she whipped out a phrase book and let them have it in
Serbo-Croatian,** word spread, and they let her stray about un-
mauled for the remaining days she had in Rovinj.

*See **wall**.

**"*Varate se asko mislite da su mi džepovi puni novčanica.*" "If you
think my pockets are lined with banknotes, you are mistaken."

POCKETS

The future ran past
with a hole in its pocket
and gold standards nailed
to its knees.

"and gold standards nailed to its knees"
    It eventually met up with the hypochondriac at a clinic in
Switzerland. They both beat it as fast as they could, faking speedy
recoveries. The place was crawling with middle-aged matrons and
blushing young grandmothers all suffering from a peculiar set of
symptoms becoming more virulent long after marriage and child-
birth but apparently related to their having had too many gold
stars plastered to their foreheads when young. This, anyway, was
the only thing the puzzled doctors could determine these patients
had in common aside from the usual things such a collection of
women might share.

POCKETS

I live in a pocket of misery
lined with shredded silk.

"a pocket of misery"
    Yolanta, of her hovel in the Marais or life in general, come to
collect 200 francs for "La Mode et la muse" from the editor of
Passion.

                    ⌐ ⌐

200 francs for
two small tickets!
Two small tickets
tripping down the
street like
skeletons with pockets.

"200 francs for two small tickets!"
    From a bilingual dream Yolanta's first night in London after a
channel crossing by Hovercraft. The second, French half went:

> *Comme être approchée d'un avenir*
> *qui est un squelette avec des poches.*
> [Like being approached by a future
> that's a skeleton with pockets.]

Pockets play a poignant part in the final scene of *The Little Match
Girl*, too. When they find her frozen body the following morning,
they discover a note in her coat pocket reminding her to mend her
pocket.

POCKETS

(from *The Gingerbread Variations*)

For my dead brother
has no hands
to put in them.

"*dead brother*"
   Gretl, again assuming the worst. Actually, his hands were quite busy working over the witch's trapezius and quadratus before the nightly frolics began.

PURSE

An old lady gets on the bus and rubs her commodious white leather purse against my arm. It feels pleasant, but I give her a dirty look just to let her know I know that I've been aggressed by a dead cow carrying her eyedrops and handkerchief.

From Yolanta's little book *Carnet,* of bus and *métro* rides the ten yellow tickets took her on. Hence the Erotic Transport of **bra**. The book was a beautiful handmade object sold to collectors, and published and painted by Passera in Caen.

RAIN

Torquil, I know that these all-embracing desires are just
asking for trouble, that it's better to begin in the glass of
water, which can shatter, spill over, be taken in to the last
liquid moment, be knocked over, refilled, have something
else poured in. Who knows? A rainstorm can fall into a
glass, and the things that happen after the storm has passed.
I wanted to add something to your life, which is not the same
as replacing what isn't already there. There's the touch,
clash, or fusion with each other and making something of it
alone: the intensity leaps onto synapses not our own and the
hunger (mine, anyway) goes out. When I give myself to you,
I am suddenly everyone's woman, as anyone can see, after
you've gone, if I wade out into the streets with this back-
wards waterfall rushing through me, from the sidewalk and
my shoes. The hunger is a delight. And thank you for lunch
in the dying light, your self to drape mine over in the coffee
and dusk of an outdoors wider than that terrace seemed to
say, for listening, for telling me. If, next time, there's anything within reach, a glass, you, I'll take it, I'll be with you,
much taken, as always.

> *found on floor by*
> *window: a DARK feather*

> Jonquil

There must have been another man in Jonquil's life:

> I thought of you.
> It rained hard for one minute.
> I thought of him.
> The roof began to leak.

REAL

You don't think I'm not real when I'm
kidding, and you don't want to believe
I am real when I'm not.

"when I'm kidding"
    Yolanta, having a bit of epistemological fun with the boys at the
Préfecture de Police, mugging in front of the camera, making eyes
at their superiors, and offering to show them her tattoo instead of
revealing her name.

"I am real"
    As an exposition of *clitoris*, this curious image crops up in *Don
Juan Is a Woman*:

> A piece of real estate. The
> owner hollers in a back room.

RING

(from *The Shattered Glass Slipper: Reflections in a Broken Shoe*)*

I pulled on my rings and blue stockings and spent the rest of the afternoon clanking about in my costume jewelry, knocking them off their feet with bons mots and aperçus, clinking my high heels together, and wishing I hadn't come.

*A subvariant of *The Glass Shoe*.

SALT

On a recent Sunday afternoon, the contents of my refrigerator included not much more than the drowsy greenness of wild ponies and a milliner, a dressmaker, a dancer, and a singer.

This was unfortunate, because when they were alive, they had run a souvenir shop in Ostend full of bric-a-brac salted with the North Sea, and skeletons warming themselves at the stove.

"a milliner"

Before winding up in someone's Sunday brunch, she managed to complete a collection of twentieth-century literature hats (see **hat**) and a big picture hat for the restless young bride in **dress**, whom she suspected of being every inch the aficionado of cheap thrills long before people started talking, and even avoiding her. Funny to find her, the milliner, in the tableau vivant of Ensor's childhood, as it was his self-portrait in plumed hat that had decided her on her calling and rescued her from those chilly studios where she posed and shivered for so little money and began so many hopeless liaisons with sensitive and penniless young men.

"a dressmaker"

No, it's not Elsbeth, who, at the time, was rereading a postcard from Czechoslovakia that had arrived on Saturday from her niece.

SALT

(from *The Glass Shoe*)

By the time the *huevos rancheros* arrived at the sleepy hacienda, we had eaten enormously off the platter of sunrise, tickled the *banditti* gagged and bound in a corner of the patio, and licked the rims of salt from each other's tequila'd lips.

"from each other's tequila'd lips"
    In another splinter of the Cinderella story, she "clattered across the dusty highway through tumbleweeds in her hand-blown Mexican glass slippers." Was Cinderella at the hacienda, then, licking the wounded *banditti* and drinking margaritas from a salted glass shoe? In Venice, she wore shoes of Murano glass, and from the Bridge of Sighs on her still unsubstantiated honeymoon, saw a girl with runaway red shoes kicking a gondolier in the head.

SATIN

Thinking himself home alone with his thoughts, and finding one of them painful beyond human endurance, the recluse raged among his cushions as he recalled the taste of satin and the mannequin's unclaspable *désinvolture*.

S C A R

Brushing against a nail on the deck chair in which the mil-
lionaire had propped her, the dummy, no longer in diamonds
and furs, but in yachting togs, and looking rather pale,
scraped her muslin* kneecap, ripping it open and getting a
bit of rust on her white skirt. She stared out at the Carib-
bean, not green like the promises—but had anything been
like he'd painted it, after their first few weekends at country
inns, where it had been so awkward sharing bathtubs with
strangers down the hall?—and several loops of stuffing came
twirling down her shin. Cotton socks, shredded libretti, and
ancient manuscripts were the stuff she was made of, stories
lacing through each other, sometimes getting tangled there,
beneath her skin (which someone had once disdainfully or
insensitively referred to as her upholstery)—about a passion
in *The Black Forest* (sort of a Wagnerian opera but all mixed
up with Greek and Roman myth, and who knows what sort of
children this coupling might produce; Pan pipes, shepherds'
flutes, Orpheus tiptoeing around the cypresses, but then this
very *gemütlich* feeling taking over not only the amatory but
also the musical theme); an Albanian having trouble with his
map; and other histories from beyond that sullen sea.

Well, she would have to wait till he carried her back to
their cabin before calling the seamstress, a soft-focused
Croatian on holiday, to come in and read her these "scraps of
the narrative handkerchief," as she called her insides, before
tucking them back into the fabric of her being and apologizing for the scar this would leave.

---

*This made life easy, because she could do her laundry and bathe
all at once, tossed into the tub, fully clothed, with some very mild
soap and *cold* water, or else the colors of her eyes might bleed, and
no girl would want to be seen with her irises bolting down her

cheeks, or any of her other markings in places where they had no right to be.

"no longer in diamonds and furs"
She was last seen in literature occupying a coveted seat in an opera house. Neither the same season nor city as the penguin's night out in **watch.**

"muslin"
The exalted role muslin has played in art and the warping and woofing of language is given more elaborate treatment in *Frangipani's Pajamas* than you are dying to let me tell you about here.

"ancient manuscripts"
Of which a crisp page disappeared in **lips.**

"passion"
See **legs; thing.**

"irises bolting"
See **boudoir,** where she bolts into the irises.

"apologizing for the scar this would leave"
Anja's actual words were:

*"Posekotina je izlečena ali brazgotina se još vidi.
Hajd, hajde, umiri se."***

**"The cut is healed but you can see the scar. There, there, my dear."

"scraps of the narrative handkerchief"
By now it will be dawning on you what stories they are, and where Anja happened upon all these tatters she's been piecing together for you.

SCARF

And then came winter, with her raw hands, her blue lips, her angora scarf lashed raffishly about her scraggy neck.

"*And then came winter*"

One reason for these cruises of Anja's was to escape the influenzas that visited her country* this time each year, and things were no better in Paris (see **fur**) or Morocco, and God knows what she might pick up from some sad case in a Swiss sanitorium, so she took to the placid seas with their languid, shufflebored passengers and the phosphorescences dancing upon waves an evening stroll on deck might reveal, at the sign of the first snowstorm, or chill of the first blasting wind.

*In *Frangipani's Pajamas*, "a plague of Reason broke out and was ravaging the country, snatching little girls right out of their pinafores and mudpies, and shoving them into bookkeeping classes before they could even brush their bangs off their furrowed little foreheads or finish the arabesques of candy hearts and raisins upon which they had been so intent."

SCARVES

In their white scarves, dark glasses, and dirty Cadillac, they sat idling on the lowest level of the parking structure (she reading a map, he keeping his eye on the windshield and a firm grip on the wheel) until the last traces of gasoline had been exhausted and the scenery dissolved.

SCHMATTE

(from *The Glass Shoe*)

I scratched my schmatte and
proceeded with the floor.

Cinderella, or Cendrine, as she is called in *Cendrine and the Garçon Flambé*, a video by Jean-Jacques Passera, picked up a few Yiddish expressions from the shops in the village, so it is not surprising to come across entries in her diary like: "I was polishing the tsatskelehs when the doorbell rang and I opened the door to a dwarf selling hairbrushes" or "I schlepped my bucket up the front stairs to do Agfa's room, but her door was locked and a sign that read MUSE PLEASE dangled from the doorknob, so I figured she was at it with her pathetic fallacies, and tiptoed off for *une petite somme* in the attic instead."

SHADOW

(from *The Gingerbread Variations*)

In those days it was bitter cold when the angels talked to a fellow at night as his shadow paused to listen for a way out of the woods.

"Hansel, what hast thou done with thy sister?"

"Ah, scattered her bones to make the trip home easier."

Now don't start dabbing at your eyes with your handkerchief. This was only one of Gretl's fantasies as she lay awake at night in the witch's bedroom wondering, after what she'd just been through, how their story would ever end, and took into consideration the treatment experience had taught her to expect from her brother. "Cowering at an indecent angle" is how she summed up these childhood memories of his humiliations when she was grown and had children of her own clambering over her lap.

"scattered her bones"

Sometimes passages of *The Gingerbread Variations* look like they're treading on Nichevo's toes, as in this scene for the corps de ballet:

Lovely in verdant underwear   the callous and grizzled
dandies waltz beside their bones. The timid stitch tuxedos
    gamble away their siestas   mate in rotundas of
gingerbread . . .

SHOES

(from *The Red Shoes*)

Actually, she quite liked these nights spent at the cobbler's, and it was even whispered in the village that she deliberately scraped them knocking into things and wore them out faster than such knocking about could account for just so she could fall asleep exhausted in the cobbler's arms with the smell of shoe polish filling her quiet breathing and shining the footgear of her dreams, her lips parted and her right fist jammed against her cheekbone* as the clocks sounded in the *horlogerie* next door.

*Her fine cheekbones were already emerging as a strength in her features, the way they lifted her face out toward the temples and cradled her dark eyes. This is something that does not always show in a girl during those years when her flesh seems to be rearranging itself every other day, modeling itself to the skeletal structure and the shape of womanhood trying to find the form, and settle into it, that this particular female will inhabit for the rest of her life—now grabbing with handfuls at her hipbones, now swelling out her calves, suddenly snapping her into a pliant sapling, crushing her into tiers of anguished tissues, then rolling her up in a mattress** and sending her off to her husband's house. But Red Shoes had a precocious face.

**The mattress at the cobbler's was made for one large person, which he certainly was, but her young and supple body made room for itself as she slipped into his embrace and sought his caresses, her cries holding onto him melting through the clocks on the other side of the yes and she was reaching the other ⠀⠀her hair slapped across his face ⠀⠀the air ⠀⠀and chest ⠀⠀jerked back over her shudders before she crashed onto his ample surface and lay twitching in the laughter rising out of her hunger that hovered over the room of shoes all laced up and nowhere to walk through her sudden stillness for once and at last and again

SKIN

The special guest of the skeleton.

One of the "tidings from Timofey," whiling away Eternity with his own lexicon, haunted by a line from Tarkovsky's *Nostalghia*: "To light up like a word, posthumously."

SKIRT

(from *The Little Match Girl*)

It was not always matches I had to offer to whoever was happening by my outstretched hand. After the holidays it was tulips—yellow, red, and cream. The rich tones of these cream tulips especially pleased me and drew me into them, down to the drop at the center where all thickness and warmth seemed to rest and begin. These flowers, at once goblets and bright or pale flames, do not really have faces or skirts. They are interiors folded back and falling into themselves. I don't care about the sexual significance of all this, and the comparisons men have made between my opening to their mouths and the trembling of rose petals at dawn as the beast of day comes to drink from them. I am rather inaccessible as a woman, being more like a cross between a small girl and a man, which is confusing to others to discover in my hesitant and possessing embrace—while mistaking me for the very embodiment of how they have always wished to be desired. It is true that there is this want dragging around in me, and that no one can help but attempt to feed it, and because I am sweet and this state of pleasure in abeyance pours off me almost continually though I am ill at ease and shabbily clothed, everyone finds himself entering with pleasure also into this hunger and allowing himself to be completely devoured.

SLEEP

Morpheus, your presence wraps around my past, the gift you found me in. Now that you're the present, it brushes past history and various outrageous misfortunes for the future and paints the way into the clearing where the only entanglement is ours. And even while the brim of each tiny wound dawned on me, there was somehow less pain, this time, in your love, which made me stay up outside all night after leaving you a note that said, "You've left my body purring so loudly the sound is keeping me awake." Specific sadnesses are spreading into a lazier, more vaguely inherent one. When I speak of places I want to sleep with you, it's not to summon dreams to fill in the present, which feels so full, but to catch some of the extra moments spilling over and touching on all sides others the way your touching me gives birth to *cent mille milliards de* phantom limbs

> in phantom limbus,
> there, where the edges are blurring,
> as I had hoped we would,

K

"*where the edges are blurring*"
    In *The Little Matchbook*,* a collection of story-sketches by the little match girl, this reads: "where the edges are burning," and the edge of the page is singed.

*Found in her other pocket.

SLEEVES

Pressed between two sleeves rubbing their tweeds against her
bare upper arms, and two voices with them that scratched
several exposed sensibilities around the table and rasped at
each other across her face, she wafted her way out of the
commingling bouquets of champagne and several resinous
reds (or was it a touch of licorice teased out of an oaken
cask?) and hurled herself into a passing dumbwaiter headed
for what levels of meaning awaited her in the lower depths.

One of those celebrated birthday dinners at Chez Panisse—
although in fact she was already as low as she could go and
there wasn't a dumbwaiter in sight.

SLIP

His gnarled hand held onto her
raincoat long after she'd given
him the slip.

I hope this isn't the peasant's daughter in **tutu**. If it is, though, it
can't be her father's hand, as he was still young and fit, so her
molester would have been some old tramp who appeared at the
pantry door looking for a few days' work or a mug of kvass. If it *was*
kvass, made from rye crumbs, then this tale is closer to **babushka**
than it seems, for the blini woman was always using crumbs* every
which way in her viatic feasts. And then, Hansel and Gretl fled the
jaws of death inside the gingerbread by following the crumbs of *The
Unfinished Cookie* through the forest—a cycle recounting the reas-
suring gestures and silent reproaches of mothers from ancient to
present times. ("Her thumbprint in the oatmeal cookie!" "I know
she sees me with the eyes in the back of her headache." "The im-
placable inside mother, who won't graciously abandon me!" "He
came to an island covered with mothers," etc.) If it *was* the budding ballerina who answered the door, she was wearing her raincoat because either the roof was leaking on a rainy day or she had
been pirouetting about in her makeshift tutu and flung on the first
garment her own hand fell upon in a dark closet modesty com-
pelled her to open at the sound of the bum's rap.

*"It's nothing but crumbs!" I cried late one night when a friend
showed up to distract me from my typewriter. "*Oui, mais on peut
faire un très bon gâteau des miettes.*"**

"Yes, but you can make a very good cake* out of crumbs." The
French should be read with a Yugoslavian accent, not quite
Serbian, not quite Slovenian.

***"These notes keep unfolding in my lap, as my life moves from
café to *métro* stop to stairway, and it's all getting folded into the
cake batter, to be poured into those rattled cake pans**** you
already know about."
                                                            —from a letter then
****See **jar**.

SOCKS

Red socks beneath black piano,
play me some blue notes, baby.

"Red socks"
   The *enfant terrible* of **watch** listening to Jeremy Menuhin at
Châtelet, and very much taken with the bit of resplendent ankle
lighting up the stage.

In the wedding vows Cinderella is composing to exchange with her
prince, in lawful deadlock, his initial assent comes in response to:
"Would you trust this woman with your socks?"

SOCKS

(from *Don Juan Is a Woman*)

Don Juan is a woman because she's so curious, and she's hotter than any room she walks into, though she can't tell the difference, the way she feels the outside brushing against grabbing stroking scratching spitting on her coming in under her dress up around her knees and slowly circling them. The world is a current jolting through her, a breath opening her many mouths and pulling apart her every seamless gesture in any direction   away from her   into her   tossing her softly off her tiptoes affronting the feigned freight in her eyes   slipping her so gently out of her italics, her stammering parentheses, her gloves of lace and socks of twine. So much to go around, so many laps to land in, so many beaux jesters rocking her hoarse cries into the scarlet corners gathering at the center of the room   shaping her sleep in the *couvertures*.

"*hotter than any room*"
    See also **fever**.

"*feigned freight in her eyes*"
    Since it was she of whom was said "she's a bright, sudden train wreck on an uneventful day," perhaps a freight train was chugging across her frontal bone, headed for a collision with his train of thought.

"*her stammering parentheses*"
    Yolanta had to give quite some thought to this before deciding that it didn't really belong in her anthology of things going on between parentheses in women's literature of all time. It was roughly at *this* time that Jacob Other, letting himself into her studio on rue de Birague (she had moved from that *pénible chambre de bonne* up seven flights of stairs), discovered her, licking the

confiture de framboises (see grandmotherly note to red **boots**) off her fingers, with a bookmark between her legs.

"*socks of twine*"
   Still, she did give the work a footnote in a piece she wrote for *Passion* called "La Mode et la muse":

> "In *Don Juan Is a Woman*, she is wearing gloves of lace and socks of twine. *Twine* twists into *entwine*, and other ways of disporting about a lover's body, or how a bougainvillea can carry on with a drainpipe."

"*hoarse cries into the scarlet corners*"
   See the crescendo of **shoes**.

"*shaping her sleep in the* couvertures"
   See the unravaged solitude of **mood**.

SOUP

Salut! I wandered out of my hotel this morning looking for a place to get warm, wound up at Beaubourg, whose bubbles are filled with sadness already despite the structure's youth. A disintegrated, ravaging need has rubbed against it too desperately; the brightness has been snuffed out, and only fatigue remains. Here in the Bibliothèque (a place where the homeless find chairs, or, if none are left, arrange themselves in lumps along the walls), a man beside me is mumbling to himself in Bulgarian as he heavily thumbs his way through a dictionary that looks like a thick Balkan soup. He wheezes and gasps between each word; the rest of us sharing his strange guttural dinner table exchange unknowing looks. I'll be in New York in April. See you there over a bowl of borscht at that Ukrainian place by the Village Gate.

—*T'embrasse,*
Yolanta

"through a dictionary"
    Not *this* dictionary, Absinthe to Zipper, abounding though it is in Balkan ambience.

SPARKLE

(from *The Little Match Girl*)

So I pulled over to the side of the
road and sparkled for a while.

STAMPS

There were always a few overseas postage stamps swimming around in his sperm. His first love had been a Swedish ex-change student, and he never quite got over her.

Jonquil, with an airplane wing stuck to that soft spot on her inner-most thigh, finally brought herself to mention to Torquil that she felt she did deserve, by their third weekend together, after all, some explanation for this phenomenon.

STARS

(from *The Little Match Girl*)

I had this silk scarf* wrapped around my face but it was damp
from my tears and then frozen and so it was stuck to me in a
most unpleasant way. My eyelashes were also encrusted with
fresh snowflakes, each a miracle of the theretofore never
expressed never to again occur, right there, on my own eyelashes—it was an awesome thought and made me appreciate
each second ticking by, for each of these, too, was like none
other, no matter how long I gazed through this same pane of
glass with a whiteness all around me and so much night yet
to come.

*The silk scarf, a deep blue square bordered by tight metallic stars,
as if the stars had been thrown out to the edge of day and were
waiting to scatter over its fields once again, I found one morning
on my doorstep, folded and refolded into a thick rectangle and
tucked into one of my own matchboxes with a note in a large,
careful, muscular hand.**

**No, this is not one of the hands I now had tossed over my shoul-
der, and I might add here that it was so cold—maybe this will give
you some idea of how cold it *was*—that I wanted to cover my fur
hands with gloves. One by one I took them into my own hands and
rubbed them and breathed on them just as the man I buy my vegetables from once did with mine*** when my blue hand held out
to him a coin in exchange for some leeks and potatoes I intended
to glorify in a shepherd's pie.

***This is one of the most touching things anyone has ever done
for me, perhaps because it was so immediate a response to a very
real condition. It wasn't as if he had been staying awake for nights
wondering what he could possibly do for that wretched creature
robbed of her girlhood by poverty and a father who punished her
with or for his own sorry lot and self-hatred—and I smiled up
gratefully at him with all my being as it engulfed his warmth.

STOCKINGS

Not only was her memory as sheer as her stockings, but each thing it held shone through every other one so vividly that all were hopelessly suffused. A street in midtown Manhattan ran through a pitcher of Löwenbrau she'd once shared with Dragomir Mirković on the banks of the Rhine so that one of its street lamps lit up the foam as it touched his lips, and a look he had given her later yet that evening stabbed the hard heart she had turned on him two years afterward in Salzburg in such a way that the blood poured into her empty glass on that same table as he offered her another round of beer and imagined the child she would bear him if all went according to his plans.

STOCKINGS

Loneliness: An emaciated woman who stands on the sidewalk with a furled umbrella saying to everyone who walks past her, "I'm awfully sorry to have to be saying good-bye to you." She looks like Mad Meg in Breughel's painting with her hair pulled back, wears pale grey stockings, and has big feet. She's standing on them. And who wouldn't? It's going to rain.

STOCKINGS

The mermaids may not have had legs, but every now and then on a slow afternoon they liked to sprawl on the rocks pretending they did, swapping isometric exercises to keep their thighs firm and shapely, complaining about their cellulite or varicose veins, and saying things to one another* about the day's catch like, "And what did your fishnet stockings drag down this time?"

*Their phosphorescent chatter was not limited to fantasy append-
ages and garments they'd never seen. The mermaids reveled in a
very rich oral tradition drawn from the flora and fauna of their
aqueous underworld, so one of them might say, halfway through an
anecdote about a tiff with some pal: ". . . and then her eyes turned
the color of barking seals, and she stormed off into a bed of kelp to
sulk and call me names I won't repeat."

SWEATER

Today I went to the Museum of Costume and Fashion to read Diderot through clothes—"La Littérature et la mode." The place was full of old ladies knitting sweaters on benches and gabbling in the foyer while Emma Bovary's wedding was being enacted in a dim niche within. I should have helped myself to one of the clicking needles! I need some layers of wool to bundle me through the rest of this winter, and cannot stand the "*Vous désirez?*" that greets me in every shop, turning so swiftly, after the "*Ah, c'est une merveille, c'est tout à fait pour vous, Madame*" or "*Que c'est chouette!*" from the younger set, to the chilliest scene, the coldest shoulder if my interest in the mirror flickers—and the thin lips press together into a slit of avaricious malice as the sweater is coolly taken from my hands.

One of the postcards home to her jar, confidante and guardian of some of Yolanta's best-kept secrets, from the weeks of research for "La Mode et la muse." Several years later she raided the jar and several friends' drawers to reconstruct her mapped and tattered winters of hovels and esplanades.

TABLE

She sat at a small round flat cracked marble table with too
many adjectives around her in one of those cafés by the sea.

Parts of this cracked table have been lost, but some intermittent
sentences were retrieved before the demitasses and glasses of water
were cleared away:

> Across the street a cement mixer grinding out its thick song.
> Someone, who sounded like a man, chuckled to himself on
> the radio, and a chorus of female voices behind him con-
> firmed his private, loudspeakered mirth. . . . The coffee came,
> and with it the waitress's legs and halfhearted hopes for a
> decent tip. . . . She waited for the coffee to cool, playing up
> the Nolo Me Tangere of the unaccompanied woman with an
> exaggerated absorption in her book. . . . All this took place
> under the gaze of a perfect stranger sitting two tables away.
> Strangers are always so perfect, she sighed, until they strike
> the first match, until they face up to the menu, until they see
> what a bitch I am.

TABLE

Like corners torn from four other tables, they would come together for dinner to rub their ragged edges across each other over bowls of bubbling *ragoût*, glasses of not so spritely Beaujolais, and tales of their childhoods they could never finish because there was nothing for dessert.

TEETH

(from *The Gingerbread Variations*)

Eyes darted like nervous beads in the hazel bushes and traced
glints of small animal appetites over the forest bed, and the
lost children breathed softly through scenes of squeaking
carnage, sharp teeth ripping into fine sinews, the crunch of
tiny bones. The beast of dawn did come at last and put an
end to all this slaughter, bringing with him the more relaxed
chomping sounds of herbivores, and low-slung quadrupeds
who rummaged among the scrubby foliage for nuts and seeds
and dense little fruits. Bees appeared from nowhere and stuck
their feet into newly opened flowers, brushed them off on the
doormats of others, returning still dusty with pollen to the
hives that belonged to the odd, tall woman with hair like
honey and an outrageous outfit she donned to plunder the
golden centers of their glutinous homes.

Long past dawn slept Hansel and Gretl, until the sun had
risen high above the chirring trees, warming the earth and
the two entwined bodies growling with hunger for berries,
hot muffins, and fresh cream. But they had hours of famished
stumbling to get through before the fateful stuffing with
scented cakes.

"breathed softly"
This implies a long night of uninterrupted sound sleep, and it
wasn't that way for Gretl at all. For hours they had followed a very
talkative stream in and out of shadows and sunlight, and she had
repeatedly lowered her muzzle into the current to guzzle its delightful waters and watch spiders skating across her reflected face, bits
of twig or leaf riding over her eyebrows and cheeks. So all through
the night and early morning she kept having to lift Hansel's arm
from around her waist, lay it gently down, and get up to pee in the
moonlight flowing over them "like Walter de la Mare's undershirt,"

she thought the first time she had awakened in this lovely embrace, snug as two gingerbread cookies fresh from the oven and
wrapped in a napkin of affection, or a dishtowel of necessity.

TELEPHONE

"You're wanted on the other
end of my whine."

"my whine"
   She also sulked, howled, whimpered, trilled: his importunate
mistress on Torquil's answering machine.

Aside from his menacing promenades, the only thing a bit strange
about the man in the red cape was his conviction that Mozart was
leaving messages on *his* answering machine.

ᴗ ᴗ

"Oh, sorry—I thought you were someone else."
"Ah, yes, I had hoped so too."

"someone else"
   From *The Wronged Number*.
   Allusions in Jacob Other's writings repeatedly graze their lips
over that extra person he carries around in his name. The preface
to his collection of essays *Couplets and Breasts* demurs: "I am a man
of letters, but I am a woman of something worse."

TELEPHONE

"How's it going?"
"Fine, as long as it keeps its distance from me."

"Who are you to understand?"
"Who are you to not be understood?"

"Well, bye-bye."
"I never really hang up."
"I never really call."

A couple of the regulars of the torn **table** ("We sat around chomping on platitudes"*) indulging in a meaningful midmorning chat.

*Whereas, in *Carnal Knowledge*, "we got the machinery in motion for a perfectly desultory evening of carnal non sequiturs."

THING

Bathed in moonlight and soaked in schmaltz, Hilda lay in his arms (or should she call them his legs?) on the forest floor, crooning lieder and popping gooseberries into his mouth and telling him fairy tales from her childhood of the little girl who sold her grandmother for a pot of cream and grew into a fur coat. What a gratified big girl *she* was—the clever things he could do with his cloven hoofs!

TIME

Dear Torquil,
   Now I have your clock. Is this your answer to "I want to be the time you have on your hands"? You've left your time in mine. The hands haven't stopped moving yet.
                          Love,
                          Jonquil

Someone is watching you
strapped to the back of
your life.

Another of the entries from beyond the grave in Timosha's pocket dictionary. See skeletons with **pockets**, Yolanta's double-entendu London dream. There is cause for conjecture that something was gnawing at the bones of his departed conscience; under *remorse* we find: "Stacked up like laundry in hell."

TOOTHBRUSH

(from *The Telltale Toothbrush*)

It was the time of Dentyne, a time when all you wanted was a pair of clean teeth, and many, even women, could not brush after every meal.

᭒ ᮿ

"There's nothing personal about my life.
Lay off my toothbrush, you creep."

TOOTHBRUSH

(from *The Glass Shoe*)

I know I've been difficult, obstinate, irascible, recalcitrant,
and hardly ever nice, but how else can I behave, in accor-
dance with the laws of my heart? I should never see the
prince again, as I think he, too, understood tonight in the
shattered smile I turned on him when he left me at my door.
What the door was in the act of disclosing: my disappearance
from his side. Yes, I wanted him to leave me here. It was
apparent how things would go this evening from the moment
he handed me the orchids and I said, "Thanks, I'll brush my
teeth with them," and stuck them in a jug above the bath-
room sink. During dinner he kept laying his napkin over my
hands and then humping them with his and drinking from
my glass. He assured me that he loved me absolutely and
without conditions, and I listened respectfully and, with
grave doubts, smashed my meringue with the back of his
spoon.

TORTE

I've been torted!

The chalet we had rented in the Zillertal turned out to be haunted by a Viennese pastry chef and we had to change our plans, so we crossed over the Dolomites and continued on to Bled. It was awful! About two or three o'clock we'd be awakened by the scents of chocolate and raspberries whooshing over the eiderdown, and then a snuffling sound, followed by lips smacking and a soft groan of gustatory pleasure, would be emitted not far from our bed. Well, you can just imagine the paroxysms of terror and desire this sent us into night after night. Running out of room, these damn postcards, see you in late August, bye for now. Aren't these cobblestone streets cute? Ha! Ask my D'Orsay pumps about that!

Yolanta

TOUCH

"Does that feel good?"
"It's putting a small dent
in my misfortune."

"a small dent"
    This comeback to Torquil some time between breakfast and bed
during a holiday tryst recalls Jonquil's cycle of autoerotic poems,
starting in a 1953 Thunderbird and grinding to a halt on a taxi ride
through Central Park—particularly one titled "Trade":

> We're in the auto trade.
> He masturbates while I bang
> out his dents.

It's a reversal of the actual proposition she refused: a guy comes to
her door offering to do some body work on the battered black
Peugeot in front of her house in exchange for—well, he just stands
there exposing her to himself with an omnivoraciously lowering
gaze.

There *is* something to be said for doorways, front porches, and
steps. In *The Glass Shoe*, we find not only the dwarf with his bag
of boar bristles, but murmurs like this in the notebook beside
Cinderella's bed:

> "It was definitely a day to lie about on one's doorstep, licking
> one's wounds or one's lollipop."

TOWEL

(from *The Toes of Nichevo*)

It pattered about the room indiscreetly,
calling for sausages, beer, a towel to dry
its feet.

The Toes of Nichevo
    Originally presented as a ballet, then as a radio play.
    Not all the terpsichorean quality was sacrificed in the rendering
for the BBC. The ballet was translated into poetic language by
Yolanta, who was hard up for money in London at the time.

> The oldest puppeteer hastens me to his gristle.
> Alone we enter the discothèque of the shoeshine
> of the moon. Alone we dance.

And much more of the same sort of stuff.

TOWEL

Oh, how she loved to stand about the lobby of an afternoon,
nabbing at passersby with her chronic cheerfulness, snapping
her bright voice at them like a towel!

"snapping her bright voice"
    Her daughter had to send her to Switzerland, where she became
one of the hypochondriac's reasons for checking out so soon.

From Timofey, glossing over nothing in his amaranthine alphabet:

> What are tears?
> Lock your face in a
> closet full of towels.

TRUFFLE

(from *La Vie in the Wild Forest* , chapter 14: "The Truffled Pig")

There was once a large adolescent male pig who had been trained since sucklinghood practically to hunt truffles in the forest in France of course. Life was not pleasant for this pig, who was mostly black with some large white elliptical spots, for he was often beaten by the truffle merchants. They were a rude, swarthy bunch with gruff voices and unendearing ways. They weren't even nice to women. They always carried large tree branches and gave the pig sound swats on his handsome mottled back and his dusty flanks. His flanks were dusty from his work in the forest, and his snout was a caked mess of dank earth gone dry in the sharp autumn air. The pig was not ex-actly unhappy, or so he preferred to think of it, but one day more than usually brilliant with white-and-blue slow motion and glints off evergreens he took his snout out of the ground long enough to start wandering through a particularly beguil-ing section of woods, and happened before long upon a hut like the Baba Yaga houses in Russian fairy tales: that is, it stood on legs, chicken legs, and turned on them, and this house talked to itself sometimes. Well, wouldn't you? Out the front door, which was not exactly closed, came an old man on skinny legs that looked like they were running even when he was walking quite slowly. He wore a long white T-shirt with variegated spots on it and that was all, had wild hair and rosy cheeks. The pig, having read Edith Sitwell on English eccentrics, recognized him straight off as a hermit, and not the kind you chain to a rock beyond your back door. The hermit, who sometimes called himself Henri, welcomed the pig with unencroaching glee and made it quite clear with few words and many gestures that he might make his home there. True harmony came easily once the pig routed out a place for himself and recounted his sordid tale. The hermit goes on with his quiet life, reading movie magazines and writing fan letters to his favorite stars, and the pig is free to roam the forest with his nose in the air and eat the hermit's cassoulet, to which, when he's feeling like it, he occasionally contributes a truffle.

T-SHIRT

(from *The Red Shoes*)

Elsbeth never gave a thought to bringing out a line of Hans
Christian Andersen T-shirts, even though she knew someone
who knew someone who knew him, and through this chain of
acquaintances found herself making him the jacket* he wore
on his rambles through Italy with an uncle or grandfather of
Karen Blixen; and he'd pounced on the story of her niece's
shoes and twisted it into a depressing, moralizing Protestant
sermon while the child herself was off on the road to the
Balkans giving an eyeful to a tavern of merchants all eastward bound with their flasks of schnapps, or brandy made of
whatever Mother Nature had deposited on their summer hill-
sides, and the goods they would be unloading in exchange for
silks and spices somewhere in the Orient.

---

*Yolanta, whose literary delusions were wrapping more and more
cozily about her own person, started dressing up in dust jackets
when the nip of autumn arrived in Paris, and it was thus she was
attired the morning the *boulanger* darted a disbelieving glance at
her feet in **bread** and wondered if The Girl Who Trod on the Loaf
had come to Paris, too, recalling that the Andersen tale begins
". . . and of how she came to a bad end," for he was having a bout
of homesickness for his native Dordogne, and the City of Light
seemed a dubious fate for him and his wife and this nice girl of
Polish descent.

T-SHIRT

T-SHIRTS OF BYZANTIUM

To W. B. Yeats:

This is no country for old men.
It's a place where little gold
parking lots are kept.

The one to W. B. Yeats, who, during his Crazy Jane period, liked
to romp about in the high winds on moonless nights wearing his
MAUD'S GONE T-shirt and wishing the circus animals, too, would
come back to his empyrean tent. This T-shirt's earlier title (now
"Driving through Byzantium"), before the grimy veneer was
removed from its gilded surface, was "Céline to Byzantium." About
the narrative I've been haranguing you with, Céline might well
have added to whatever else you're thinking: "She was waxing
devilish eloquent. The hope of extricating herself from this shady
mess at last was making the old bitch* lyrical after her own filthy
fashion."

*See note to **table,** the one at the seaside café, not the one with
Beaujolais stains on a white tablecloth and dessert spoons waving
in a circle** of gesticulating hands.

Don't see **circle. At the most one of them would have thought
to bring along a stash of toffee in his pocket to see him through the
interminable sessions of soul-baring he attended only because the
cook was quite good. They soon stopped inviting him, anyway,
when his comments diminished to a laconic "UMM. UMM."—a
favorite line of his from a Mishima play, but not the sort of empa-
thy one was expected to exude at these things.

TUTU

(from *The Red Shoes*)

The cobbler's shop, a mere shoebox clamped between the
tailor's and the *horlogerie*, had wooden feet that squatted in
the window like stunned ducks; devices that squeezed and
whirred; little drawers full of nails that looked old and shiny;
unattached heels that knew nothing yet of aimless wandering; and shelves from floor to ceiling with pairs* of boots and
shoes waiting to be reclaimed.

*The cobbler did not like it if someone brought in one shoe all by
itself. Sometimes a peasant would walk for miles with one disorga-
nized boot in his hand, the one not holding his wayfarer's lunch of
sheep's milk cheese from Corsica wrapped in pimientos and *herbes
de Provence*, a good crusty bread, with a sole worn through or coming unstitched and pulling away from the rest of the foot; or a toe
cracked from sloshing and standing in mud, in soil cooking with
fresh manure—and this peasant, after a pleasant repast on this day
off from his own land and responsibilities and the weary, accusing
regard of his wife and the smudged faces of his children who
worked willingly enough but with faraway looks in their eyes.**

**Where his daughter got the idea of being a ballet dancer is
beyond the scope of this story's speculations, but it was heart-
rending to see her in the mock tutu she had fashioned out of an
old mail-order catalogue slip of pale pink with white laces crossing
from the waist up to her clavicles. She had installed a dance studio
in a corner of the barn from pieces of mirror found lying broken on
a heap of stained glass crates from Belgium behind the glazier's.
Along one wall ran a barre she clutched*** at as one foot held the
ground and the other rose and fell through arcs cut over the dusty
surface of the floor.

***He would arrive, by this time clutching the boot in the other
hand, after a half day of reveries and extensive vistas over the flat
countryside and some irritating thoughts this changing landscape
could not mollify or vanquish, and the cobbler would greet him

cordially but with discouragement, for he could not accept one shoe alone.****

****This was a mixture of mental disequilibrium, sentimentality or compassion, and guilt for being the survivor, at birth, of a pair of twins who had both shown such promise before. The other one was a girl they named Danila and dressed in petals before returning her to the darkness out of which she had barely arrived.

And so the peasant was obliged to trudge back to his farm with its fence sliding into fallible angles, the trouble with the weather, the vicissitudes of all these shoots forever pushing out of the ground, of all these pigs, cows, geese never ceasing to dance for his attention, and the damp and impatient budding beauty of his youngest child, whose good-night kisses had been recently too demanding, too prolonged.

UMBRELLA

Why do I have the impression that I am
clutching an umbrella as I fall asleep?

In my dream I am visiting a cemetery. At the entrance to the
necropolis is a library full of books on the many ways to die.
But they are, of course, the ones we've been reading, and the
ones we are about to begin.

"a library full of books"
  Yolanta's dream, exquisite corpse.

UNDERSHIRT

You come blundering through my dreams
with your undershirt on upside down and
your Tierra del Fuego cologne.

"your Tierra del Fuego cologne"
    Torquil did go off to Patagonia "to try and forget" soon after
Jonquil had dumped him on his own doorstep and abandoned herself to that other tempestuous affair.

UNDERSHIRT

Home from another Sunday drive in the parking structure,
with their exhausted clothing tumbling among lost socks and
soap, they sat in the laundromat playing strip poker, she
starting with the charms of her bracelet, he moving on to his
undershirt, after, of course, his curlers, and the pink hairnet
flashing with sequins that matched his chamazulene eyes.

"their exhausted clothing"
      See **scarves.**

"lost socks and soap"
      This would intimate things lost on you and me to the muslin
dummy in **scar.**

"playing strip poker"
      The game continues in *Frangipani's Pajamas*, but the stakes and
players are changed, and it's set in a seraglio.

"flashing with sequins"
      In Bedruthan's story of **comb,** a mermaid is sewing sequins onto
her tail. Or am I sewing sequences onto my tale? I just exhumed
one fluttering little scrap from the pale author, too: "Ask not for
whom the tale is told. It's told by me."

"chamazulene eyes"
      The only reason his eyes are so identified is the shampoo made
from this rare flower so recently rinsed from his lustrous hair, the
luster, I suppose, owing to the African Butter Herb in the formula.
The one time Anja had given Morocco a whirl, she drank a tea of
Moroccan blue camomile to calm a queasy stomach—a lovely blue
liquid glistening in an icy glass on a terrace with too much sun.

WALL

On her way back from doorstep of death, she paused to consider biting the wall.

All she'd really been after was "a complete rest from the worst of life for the better part of the time," her suicide note said. The wall wasn't even made of gingerbread, so she had second thoughts about that, too.

Jacob Other amplifies this interpretation *and* suggests an alternate reading:

> "She" is a little playmate of the Girl Next Door (see the final **door**), and a precocious purveyor of Girl Scout cookies who'd read Kafka's "A Hunger Artist" at an impressionable age; or this same child was simply skipping home from her chum's, her stomach growling, after an afternoon of Little Richard, Buddy Holly, and "Chantilly Lace."

WATCH

(from *The Little Match Girl*)

I took one of the fur hands into my own and held it by the
wrist to read its pulse. The loud ticking of the Swatch watch
I'd bought on rue de Rivoli was distracting, mixing its ticks
up with the beat of the blood, so I pressed its face against my
back and muffled it in my coat. The beat seemed sluggish to
me, but I don't know how to correlate these things with
blood pressure, metabolic changes in subzero temperatures,
degrees of wakefulness, and the presence of light, of which
we have so little in this circumpolar region. I do recall once
hearing about the grim struggles of the penguin to keep his
metabolism intact, and the picture of his life painted against
that blasting white background did much to allay my mis-
impression about the intrinsic comicalness of these birds,
and affected my feelings about the amusing behavior of one
of our *enfants terribles* at the Opéra. Not wishing to wear
tails himself one night, he appeared in his box with a penguin at his side, shifting it to his knees after the entr'acte,
and cradling the sleepy Sphenicada in his arms through the
final scenes of *La Bohème*, for the barblessly feathered visitor
was overwhelmed by the warmth thrown off from tiers of
bejeweled torsos emerging from fur wraps and heavy scents
and curls.

"and heavy scents"
    The penguin was not put off by scented or bejeweled torsos per
se. *Au contraire*, one of his most ardent pursuits those first euphoric
few weeks in Paris had been waddling around the Faubourg St.
Honoré with a lady friend who permitted him, *"avec plaisir, chéri,"*
to atomize her pulse points with his own selections, bending over
his shiny black head or holding him up to her throat and listening

to his cries of approval or disbelief. So, this evening at the Opéra, before the mélange drove him completely out of his senses, he was able to distinguish, with the satisfaction of the budding connoisseur, such fragrances as Demimonde, Fleurs du Malheur, Grosse Bête, Perdition, Flagrante Delicto, and a new one called Mazeltov that was making a big splash in the heat of the Dreyfus Affair.

WEDDING TRAIN

To the end of her days she dragged her
wedding train around with her and lived
happily ever after him.

He unfolded her for the rest of his life.

"*He unfolded her for the rest of his life*"
    In the not so intimate parallel play of another marriage, the
peasant tried to *unravel* his wife (see note to **dress**), but by the end
of the day he had little stamina for such tussles, what with getting
up long before sunrise to stagger about in a state of beatitude listening to the lowing of his wanton cows, and then roaming over
his property for hours admiring God's nimble handiwork in every
pistil, stamen, and seed, and so he abandoned himself at bedtime
to his flannel pajamas, eating pistachios, and reading escapist
metafictions like *A Doll among the Jungle*, by Jean-Jacques Passera:

> "Losing the thread of her story in the jungle, she removed the
> heroine's pith helmet and ran her smudged fingers distract-
> edly through the typewriter ribbon tangled in the runaway
> debutante's matted hair."

WIND

Just back to London by Deux Chevaux (home to a garden
shutting down for the winter, the furniture put away under
plastic, and one lonely hollyhock flower violetly nodding its
head over things going to seed) from two weeks on the coast
of Cornwall, a twelve-hour trip in the little red truck, with a
stop at Castle Drogo (Lutyens, pre-New Delhi) and a visit to
a medieval manor, Montacute, now in the tweedy hands of
the National Trust—followed by a Devon cream tea that
ruined dinner for the next two weeks (well, that's laying it on
a bit thick). London looks positively festive with its cars and
red and green lights, shop and pub signs, and its roundabouts
about which Londoners so courteously comport themselves.
Sunday afternoon, today, we strolled among other ones on
foot in Kew Gardens, where they were out catching the autumn light, and trees were burnished in red and god (gold,
but the typo stays).

In Cornwall we wandered around the countryside, had to
stop at every church, named for saints like Issy, Petherick,
Columba (a fifteen-year-old who saved her village from a
bear), and in every town and village, each with its curious
pattern of streets; and everywhere my head was blasted
through by winds, rains, clouds, some hot sunshine (during a
ten-mile hike along disappeared railroad tracks and through
fields each with the obligatory disquieting bull, and one pub
for a Smuggler's Split a brief road offered up before we clam-
bered over another wall), the sound of relentless Atlantic
waves whipped up and dashing against the rocks.

We slept like two muffins in a toaster (the caravan on
Treyarnon Bay was not much bigger than one), and when it
rained, I curled up with radio plays on the BBC, Boswell's
Life of Johnson, Cornish ghost stories, and the weekly news-
paper, mostly about cows. Even the one crime reported came

out MILK BOTTLE USED AS DEADLY WEAPON. Went to a horse auction to look at the animals and people—wild-eyed ponies, and country types with broad high cheekbones stuffing Cornish pasties into their mouths. You can walk for days along the coast, at cliff-edge, on the softest, greenest turf (just ask my bare feet, not deprived of this tactile thrill), over footpaths that have been padded upon for generations of pirates and dairymen. We lived on mushrooms picked every other day in a cow field near Bedruthan's Steps (Bedruthan was a giant who stalked through here centuries ago; his steps lead down to the sea, where once his large footprints were lapped away), crab, mussels, sea spinach growing savagely along every wall and hedge, clotted cream, toast and marmalade, and all that clean fierce air.

Yolanta

WINDOW

She lived to open closed letters, and to
loop each word through its other windows,
out of the worlds within.

See the painted envelope of whispers flying off on a carpet from
door into the next volume of the dummy's tales.

The window next to this one was written for Silvia Monrós
Stojaković, whose borzoi letter Anja quotes in her correspondence
with Elsbeth: ". . . they run in circles around the wolf trying desperately to run away in a straight line." See also the alarming wave
in note to **dress**. And the little match girl's footsteps delivering her
again and again to the wolf at the window of her death. But Anja
was discussing the art of tidy seams.

ZIPPER

The afternoon sun slid along her buttocks
like a lost zipper.

(*Note to artist:* Well, actually, I picture a Sisyphus who seems to
have forgotten what he is supposed to be doing, going uphill with
considerable difficulty and a rough stone, and instead is gliding the
sun, its glorious golden sphere, along a beautiful body lying nice
and flat and naked and curvaceously on the feverish grass.)

"uphill with considerable difficulty"
    Although the lay of the land is similar, this isn't the guy being
tormented in Jonquil's *The Mistress of Sisyphus*. And what a tease
she is, treating her lover to the same unending struggle Camus
likens to our own.

"a beautiful body lying nice and flat"
    The body of this book, intimately unappareled.

Yolanta contends that the zipper belongs to the Albanian (the lost
one—remember him?). When you open it, what you find is your
copy of this book, because it's time to read it again.

AN AFTERWORD FROM YOLANTA

As you know, from reading this unbuttoned lexicon, I am
something of a nympho-biblio-maniac. I don't care anymore
what people say about me, or what you are thinking right
now, let alone what weird pictures . . .—oh, never mind. I
shouldn't be talking about myself like this. I'm supposed to
be telling you about the book, why it's a dictionary, why it's
changed its name since the last time I popped my books into
its toasters. Long ago I decided to have the last word on this
fabrication, and after some very unpleasant scuffles with two
seamstresses over pieces pulled out of the dummy, we reached
a tussled agreement. I was to have my way with the dishev-
eled dictionary presentation while they stitched together the
ragged pieces of which each entry is composed. I don't know
who wrote the notes (I have my suspicions: two people in
Paris, one of whom you've met; you guessed it: Jacob Other),
although I consented to write this afterword only on condition that some of the notes touching my person were changed
or even effaced. Well, there was one other condition: Elsbeth
promised to mend my mauled raiments, my tattered alphabets
(I told you it was a tussled agreement) and make me some
new outfits* after I endure the poverty and deprivation of my
next appearance in literature.

This book is sort of a cross between two literary passions of
my childhood: reading the dictionary, and spending hours
with a book of cloth pages on which other pieces of cloth
were sewn, and then shoes with laces, shirts, skirts, pants,
and dresses with buttons, zippers, hooks, snaps—all the fas-
tenings imaginable to a child growing up in the innocent
days of the post-jitterbug fifties.

*Not the wedding gown! Although I'm already at work on my gift
for the newlyweds.

One thing I learned then, because it was often *The Shorter Oxford Dictionary* I was smudging with my sticky little thumbs, is that there is a story behind *every* word. Oh, I learned a lot at an early age back in those dark summer days. Like under *brim* you find:

1. intr. Of swine: To be in heat, rut, copulate
2. trans. Said of a boar 1552

Once my carnally precocious brother had enlightened me about the intransitive stuff (although his demonstration with a neighborhood playmate looked pretty transitive to me), it was that "said of a boar 1552" that intrigued me. It may well have been said of many boars in 1552, unless there was just one boar in very big demand. It's a small example, but all I mean to say is that every word, I discovered as I grew older and began to talk in compound-complex sentences and put together abstract ideas, has many stories behind it, and behind each word in each story, many more are hiding.

I think of the words in *this* dictionary as windows through which we climb into the stories onto which they open. Actually, it's the stories that open the windows. I'm not kidding. Anja, Elsbeth, and I were working in the opposite direction of the lexicographer—starting with the fragmented stories, the "said of a cup, frock, cake, etc.," and moving from the tatters of the tales toward individual words those scraps "define."

Actually, I've left out some of the negotiations, and will find myself left out of volume two if I don't briefly recount how the ultimate construction of this book was really a concerted effort of its many inhabitants. Jacob Other, who's always been unreasonably indulgent with me, used his influence to convince several hold-outs (the penguin, Sleepless Beauty, the man in the red cape, and the hypochondriac, whose gravest illness is mistrust of all living things) that I should have my way with the disarrayed dictionary trick. Anja and Elsbeth, of course, always were in charge of the stitchery, and in fact are these tales' first editors, as we don't even get to see the stuffing that they reject or have set aside for later. It was Red Shoes who insisted on footnotes and on the book careening all over the place. Cinderella argued for keeping some stories in slivers, since her shoe had been shattered by a prince dancing on the wrong foot. Fortunately for us all (you too), or we'd have wasted away, the blini woman said that the book must be well fed, and teamed up with the innkeeper's wife of **place** and the gingerbread witch, who, more *artiste* than murderess at times, provided the *patisseries*.

Here's the rest of the deal we struck: that I would relinquish all influence on the structure of the second volume, which the two seamstresses are puzzling over this very moment. They've permitted me (Elsbeth having taken a few marketing seminars) to divulge that the tales continue on their way through Czechoslovakia with Red Shoes, as her aunt feels that making the girl a star might do wonders for her affliction. But curiosity was eating at me, and one night I ransacked Elsbeth's room while she and Anja were conferring in Slovenia (Lake Bled, actually, where, as you learned from **torte**, I have also caroused) and took a look at her plans. The dear child is to be thrown into the harem in Constantinople.

That dear child brings us to the question you must be dying to ask. What's this book doing slipping out of its title and walking off in another? The truth is, it was wearing red shoes long before it got dressed, however scantily, as *Intimate Apparel*, and from the first moment of *that* book's publication, it suffered a case of mistaken identity: a genre gap. The Library of Congress was baffled and bemused, but *Intimate Apparel: A Dictionary of the Senses* was sold as a reference book, banished to a section of bookstores where no one *I* know ever goes looking for diversion, delight, and debauchery, let alone ambiguity, innuendo, and pain. Believe me, we languished there, and some slunk off to other projects or committed suicide. Timofey tried, but couldn't, since he was already dead, and he was working on his own amaranthine alphabet (see **time**), which gave him a purpose in perpetuity, a reason to go on dying. Don't worry about the penguin or the mermaids: he's become a consultant to Guerlain, and they are testing the waters of the Caspian and the Bosporus for volume two of these tales. Jonquil Mapp decided to live up to her full name and study cartography, so she's now crawling over maps as well as mattresses. As for me, I spun on my heel and tripped myself back to Paris, the story of my life. . . .

Years went by, the horizon turned black, Elsbeth developed arthritis and had to hire some nubile *modistes* with nimble fingers to do the fine lacework on the wedding dress, which was beginning to smack of Miss Havisham or Eleanor Rigby, so absurdly did Cinderella's engagement drag on.

And then along came the guardian angel of metafiction, to rediscover and recover our book, with the new cover by the visitor in **slip** and the new title putting the focus back where it belongs. It was explained to us all (called in from the four corners of the earth) that Dalkey Archive Press had been hot for these streaking shoes for quite a while, but with the clairvoyance I've noticed in many bibliophiles, did not approach us until I'd fallen for Jacques Roubaud's *Princess Hoppy*, and until Jacob, the peasant in bed (**wedding train**), a few renegade Slavic Gastronomes, and I had had our first few flings with Flann O'Brien. *The Dalkey Archive* we passed among ourselves with such abandon that it too wound up in tatters and was nearly mistaken for some of Anja's work-in-progress.

This sense of a homecoming really concerns more than one book and its many directions, for just as "The Red

Shoes" is at the heart of this book,** *The Red Shoes and Other Tattered Tales* is central to all the other books in which I appear as a significant or cameo character: *The New Well-Tempered Sentence, The Deluxe Transitive Vampire, Paris Out of Hand, Frangipani's Pajamas,* and *Through the Looking-Trap.* The Slavic Gastronomes of **lunch** fed many passages to *The Ravenous Muse.* As long as *this* book was out of print, the rest were incomplete, without a center, however strange a center it may seem. And so there's great jubilation, much smacking of lips, walking on water, clattering down steps as we all rush toward Normal, Illinois, to reassemble and fall into our new places in a harmonious arrangement.

Both because it was the tale that most needed to be told and because it contains its own source,* a catchy paradox, since the dummy is part of "The Red Shoes." Here you enter one small story on the run, and look what you happen upon—a veritable muslin sarcophagus of literature, libretti, etymologies, who's about to undergo a startling transformation herself with the commedia dell' arte troupe in Istria.

***and the source of all the other tales.

THANKS

The cast of characters who have my love and gratitude is
nearly as rowdy and intricate as the one that's been leading
you astray. Were I to cut loose with subtexts and footnotes,
we'd have another book on our hands, so I shall confine
my remarks to the principal players and write, instead, the
second volume, on its way through the Balkans.

Thanks to Grace Fretter for a house and giant closet
where the drama began; Bob Baldock for the little match
girl's fragility and for tripping my memory down Bedruthan's
Steps. Miroslav Vyletal, of the Shoe Museum in Gottwaldov,
Slovakia, was forthcoming with his collection and zeal.

Vladimir and Tanja Kasnar and Marisa Mascarelli took
me to Rovinj vicariously, till the real trip began. Silvia
Monrós Stojaković got there first to make sure we would
meet. Douglas Ernst added Baden-Baden to Yolanta's itiner-
ary and began the healing whose malady inspired *The Red
Shoes* and *The Little Match Girl.* Harvey Sachs brought on the
Toscanini pajamas; my Tyrolean cousins, The Night of the
Sachertorte. Rastislav Mrazovac took all of me everywhere,
even Kossovo, threw away my passport, and burned my
pantalons.

Barbara Hodgson played with "Comb" and "Scar" to invite
a new sense and shape. Irene Bogdanoff Romo was on hand
with her eyes, and Jann Donnenwirth also looked things over
more than once for decisions in design. Thank you in
Russian to Boris Lopatin for standing me up on his birthday, abandoning me to my grandmother and "Frock," out of
which so many of these stories unwound.

Paris has given me everything I've needed, and also Cecil
Rivoli, the *horlogerie* next door, Edison Simons, Domitilla
Flavia Cavaletti Guillerme; the *cordonnier* on rue de
Bellechasse; my chum from the Antipodes Jane de Couvreur.

A sequence of settings and inhabitants began with Andrei Codrescu and *Exquisite Corpse:* Jean-Jacques Passera, rue Dauphine, Le Village Bulgare, Danielle Mémoire, Guillaume Pineau des Forêts, and La Folletière, where Cinderella still leaves her bed unmade.

Elisabeth Scharlatt and Linda Parker-Guenzel gave me honesty and equivocation. My agent, Maia Gregory, and my mother, Camilla Collins, waved a few wands. Lisa Weber waved my wings. Carol Dunlop waved a handkerchief, after she and Julio Cortázar lifted me out of a thirty-year disenchantment.

Although the dummy still isn't saying much, Patrick Grizzell, the Sacramento Poetry Center, and Sacramento Metropolitan Arts Commission made me open my mouth and tell these tales out loud. Timothy Becher contributed a clarinet, a journey, a pair of blue boxer shorts to catch the fireman.

At a precarious moment, Thomas Christensen and Farrokh Shayesteh kept me and the book together by understanding its many directions. It was only then that it slipped on its red shoes and ran wild through forbidden territory, taking me where I longed to go. Guy Davenport brought me into a shoe shop, third century B.C., with his translation of Herondas in his essay of that name in *Every Force Evolves a Form* (North Point, 1987). From his immortal *Darconville's Cat,* Alexander Theroux loaned his death's head to adorn the girl next **door.**

Alonzo Davis and Dixie Swift set me off on the final lap to run, or was it a lap to land on? Charles Simic in more ways than one got me into the introduction, which was also a reluctant departure. Responses from readers, written to me or not, breathe new life into every word.

My two unknown grandmothers, Molly Cykler and Karen Elisabeth Munch, became the two seamstresses Anja and Elsbeth, who assembled the texts and are seeing to the wedding gown.

And at last, after many humiliations and misunderstand-ings, along came Dalkey Archive Press to let this book both out of the wrong clothes and onto the right shelf in the bookstores and your *bibliothèque*. Steven Moore has given tender ministrations and astute observations as editor and lover of these tales.

Drago Rastislav Mrazovac long ago understood that "*la fille aux chaussons rouges est universelle*"* and painted her shoes of suffering, the cost of curiosity.

*"The girl in red shoes is universal."